THE BASEBALL MYSTERY

ALSO BY NORVIN PALLAS

- The Secret of Thunder Mountain
- The Locked Safe Mystery
- The Star Reporter Mystery
- The Singing Trees Mystery
- The Empty House Mystery
- The Counterfeit Mystery
- The Stolen Plans Mystery
- The Scarecrow Mystery
- The Big Cat Mystery
- The Missing Witness Mystery

THE

BASEBALL
MYSTERY

By

NORVIN

PALLAS

WILDSIDE PRESS

The Baseball Mystery

Published by Wildside Press LLC
www.wildsidepress.com

To

David, Russell, and Lois Ann

Contents

THE BASEBALL MYSTERY

1 1,001 Things

Confusion in a newspaper office is not unusual, but one Saturday afternoon in August things seemed to have reached their ultimate in chaos. Mr. Dobson, editor of the *Town Crier,* had rented the empty office next door to the newspaper office as headquarters for the state amateur baseball tournament, and both offices were filled with activity.

Ted Wilford, college student and summertime cub reporter for the Forestdale *Town Crier,* was doing his best to be in two places at once, as he hurried back and forth between the two offices. It was largely through Mr. Dobson's efforts that the tournament had been brought to the small town of Forestdale, but the editor, his secretary, Miss Monroe, and the newspaper's regular reporter, Carl Allison, had their regular duties to perform if the paper were to come out on schedule. So the handling of the tournament had fallen to Ted.

"Sergeant Jeffers just telephoned," Mr. Dobson informed him as Ted, having obtained what he needed from the files, was about to make a hurried exit. "He wants you to stop at the police station for a minute on your way home."

"OK," Ted agreed readily, wondering what the sergeant wanted with him but he had no time to speculate upon it just then.

During one of his brief absences from the headquarters office, a wooden crate had arrived, and Nelson Morgan was at work prying off the cover with a screw driver.

"What's in there?" asked Jane Yuleson curiously.

"Frogs," Nelson informed her.

1

"Frogs! What do they need frogs for?" Jane's knowledge of baseball rules and traditions was shaky.

Nelson shrugged. "You can't have a baseball tournament without them."

Ted smiled but felt that the sooner they got started the sooner they would be finished.

"Are those the players' cards, Nel? Good, then we can get to work on them."

"You mean we have to fill out one of those cards for every player in the tournament?" asked Helen Howland in some alarm.

"That's right—but it won't take so long with several people working on them—and they don't all have to be done today."

Nelson had the cover off by now, and extracted a number of cards, handing one to each of the persons standing around him. There was room for each player's name, his team, baseball classification, where he was to be housed, and the schedule. Each team was scheduled for three games at one of Forestdale's two baseball diamonds, but it was understood that if a team lost a game, the remainder of its schedule was automatically canceled. All this was explained in smaller type on the reverse side, along with various rules and instructions for the players.

Since some of the required information for the cards could be rubber stamped, the boys were put to work at this job. Then the cards were to be handed over to the girls, who would enter the individual information. Soon they were all at work at the long tables Ted had had installed.

"With all the things to be done, Ted," Cliff Corby inquired, "how did you decide that *this* was the thing that had to be done right now?"

"What can you do? When there are too many things to think about, all you can do is pick out the most important job and get at it."

"My system's just the opposite," Cliff remarked. "I like to

get all the small odds and ends out of the way first, and then I can concentrate on the *big* job I've got to do. Small things first, I say."

"And I've tried it both ways," Nelson complained, "and *neither* way works for me."

It was of course unusual to hold the statewide baseball play-offs in such a small town, with only one hotel, and with only two suitable diamonds plus a practice field. It would have been completely impossible for Forestdale to provide housing, restaurants, and other facilities for such an invasion all at once. But Ted and Mr. Dobson, working over their plans through many an evening, had drawn up a detailed schedule for bringing the players into and out of town so that the full burden would never be felt all at one time. No one could have been more surprised—or more pleased—than they were when their plan was accepted.

"How did you ever work out that plan?" Margaret Lake asked Ted. "I don't think I understand it even yet."

"Sheer genius," Nelson replied, before Ted had a chance to answer. "You don't ask questions. You just admire him."

Monday morning's schedule called for teams coming from points at some distance from Forestdale. These players would arrive Sunday afternoon or evening, and have a good night's sleep before their games. Teams close to Forestdale were scheduled for Monday afternoon, and they could make the drive in the morning and still not be tired. Teams losing Monday morning would leave town by evening, but teams losing Monday afternoon would stay over till the next morning. There was no use giving them the "bum's rush," as Nelson expressed it, and the delay would give them a chance to look over Forestdale, become acquainted with other players, and watch a few games besides their own.

Only half the teams were scheduled for Monday. The other half would play on Tuesday. By Tuesday night half of the teams would be eliminated from the tournament, and by Wednesday the pressure on the town of Forestdale would be much relieved. The semifinals would proceed at a more leisurely pace on Wednesday and Thursday, and the finals in each class were scheduled for Friday.

"Anybody here wishing for rain next week?" asked Jim Wessox.

Of course, if there should be an all-day rain—which seldom happened at this time of year—the entire schedule would simply be moved back a day, taking in Saturday. If only a few of the games should be rained out, then the schedule would have to be improvised in the most convenient way. The real trouble would be a heavy rain early in the week, delaying the departure of teams already in Forestdale, while other teams were still arriving. If such a thing should happen, they would have to find emergency housing in the school gym and other places. Needless to say, Ted and his staff were among those hoping most fervently that there would be no rain.

"Is anyone aching for a bruise?" was Nelson's retort to Jim.

But even with the best of plans, the forty-eight teams which were to participate in the play-offs could not be housed in the hotel and the few motels lying within easy driving distance of Forestdale. Many players would stay in private homes, and nearly every house in town with an extra bedroom had been placed on Margaret's list, for she was in charge of housing arrangements. Ted's mother had been among those who volunteered to help out, and the Wilfords had been assigned two players.

"Whom did we get?" Ted inquired, when there was a little lull for both of them, and Margaret had turned back to her file.

"A pitcher and a catcher from the Class E Eagleville Eaglets," she informed him. "Their names are Larry Dodge and Cal Farmington."

"Eagleville usually comes up with some pretty good teams," Ted recalled, but he did not know enough about the players to tell whether Larry and Cal were stars of the team, or mere bench warmers. The Eaglets, as Ted learned by consulting his schedule, would be arriving late Sunday afternoon, for they had an early game on Monday morning. Like all the players, they would come with the hope of staying until the finals on Friday, though most of the boys were certain to be disappointed. If the Eaglets lost their first game, then Larry and Cal would be leaving with the rest of the team the same day, and Ted would receive two new players.

"I guess I've found a place for everyone," Margaret remarked, "if only it doesn't–" but she thought it best not to mention the possibility of rain again.

"Good for you!" Ted applauded.

"But no fooling, Ted, why *did* Forestdale get the play-offs when larger towns with better facilities were available?"

"I think they were after a small town this year, Margaret. It wouldn't surprise me if they'd had a little trouble last year they aren't talking about, and thought they could give the boys better supervision in a small town."

"I hope we don't have anything like that. Mr. Dobson is always going to bat for the kids. It would break his heart if there were any serious trouble this week after all the effort that's gone into the tournament."

"Children don't get such a good press," said Ted with a grin. "Maybe that's what bothers Mr. Dobson the most. He leans over backwards trying to be fair, but not all editors do that. He's one in a million and a great guy to work for."

"Did somebody say work?" asked Nelson, coming up to them. "Then how about getting at it?"

"Right," Ted agreed. "What about you? Have you got the baseball scoring rules all memorized?"

"Not quite," said Nelson with a grimace, "but I hope to get by." He had been appointed one of four official scorers to record the games. "I've been looking over the scoring for last year, and I think I know what they expect."

"If this is a stupid question, you can laugh," Margaret put

in, "but just what does a scorer do, and why is it important? He doesn't have anything to say about who wins the game, does he?"

"No," Nelson agreed, "that's settled by the umpires down on the field. But the scorer has to keep the individual records straight: he must decide whether the batter gets a hit or the fielder an error, what are the batting averages and earned-run averages, which are the winning and losing pitchers, and all that. Believe me, I'm going to get you girls going on your comptometers before this thing is over."

"I thought baseball was supposed to be a team game," Helen Howland joined in. "As long as their teams win, what else matters?"

"I guess baseball players are human just like everybody else," Nelson replied, "and they want to know how they performed individually, apart from the team. And if they decide to brag a little, when bragging is in order, how does that make them any different from the rest of us? But I'll tell you how scoring is *really* important. There just might be one . . . or two . . . or three players in this tournament who are going to end up in the big leagues. And don't think there won't be scouts watching them.

"The first thing a scout ever investigates about a player is his statistics as a player. Then if that seems promising, he may decide to go take a look for himself. Believe me, I'm glad I've been assigned to the lower classifications. I would rather not have the responsibility of ruling on older players who may have a chance for the big leagues."

"Ducking responsibility?" asked Cliff mockingly.

"No, but I don't think I should tackle something I'm not qualified for, either—especially if other people might get hurt."

Cliff had been placed in charge of equipment, and Jim was official grounds keeper for the two diamonds and the practice field. When Ted inquired how they were getting along, both answered that everything seemed to be under control.

"Though the grass is a little bit brown," Jim was reminded. "I could use a good r——— I mean a heavy dew."

The work moved forward, and they kept at it until six-thirty. Most of them were willing to work longer, but Ted decided to call a halt.

"No sense overdoing, and we're all tired. We'll have to open the office tomorrow afternoon for early arrivals. I'll be here by three, and I hope some of the rest of you will be able to relieve me before the day's over."

They all promised to stop in when they could, and the group dispersed. Ted refused a ride home in Nelson's car, knowing that it would delay the others, for he remembered his promise to stop off at the police station.

He found Sergeant Jeffers on duty at the desk. Though he and the officer were good friends, there was often a little tension between them, too. Ted's principal concern was to report the news, and Jeffers' was to enforce the law, so that inevitably there were occasions when each felt he was not getting as much cooperation from the other as he should.

"You asked me to stop, Sergeant Jeffers?" Ted inquired.

"Yes, I did, Ted." The telephone rang, and he was busy for a few minutes. Then he hung up, wrote a few words on a pad, and turned to Ted. "I just wondered if everyone was clear about the curfew?"

"Oh, yes." Ted pulled out one of the cards which would be given to every player. "You notice that it stresses the eleven o'clock deadline."

"That's good, Ted, although we can't count on them to read the small print."

"I think they will. These cards are sort of souvenirs."

"Well, Ted, what I wanted to ask you is to pass the word along quietly that we really intend to enforce the curfew. The movies and other places of entertainment are cooperating with us. We've sworn in a few extra officers for temporary duty, and we intend to keep the streets patrolled. We don't want to get tough, and we're not going to object to impromptu parades or snake dances or school yells or normal celebrating, but we're not going to put up with any rowdyism either."

As he walked home thoughtfully, Ted wondered if the sergeant had anything specific in mind.

2   The Invasion Begins

At three o'clock on Sunday afternoon Ted unlocked the door of tournament headquarters and went inside. As soon as a team arrived, the manager was to stop in at headquarters to register, and Ted or whoever else was on duty there would give him the cards for the players on his team. Margaret already had the small bundles arranged neatly on the desk for each team due to arrive that day. These cards would direct the boys to the places where they were to stay. Although Forestdale was a small town and it was probable that anyone could find his proper address, Ted hoped to have a few of his friends available for guides should they be needed.

But Ted's first visitor was neither one of his staff nor one of the baseball managers. It was Ken Kutler of the North Ridge *News-Record*. He came in and slumped in a chair, his long legs stretched out into the aisle.

"Everything under control, Ted?" he inquired.

"So far," Ted replied, a little cautiously, realizing the complications which still might arise.

Ken looked around the office, with its posters, telephones, typewriters, comptometers and cleared tables.

"You seem to have a pretty good system going here–probably better than I could have done in North Ridge, since I don't have a handy group of young people to rely on. I would have enjoyed being host to some of the visiting newspaper reporters, though. I owe a good many of them favors I'd like to repay."

"Do you think a good many reporters will be down here?" Ted inquired.

"Oh, yes," Ken assured him. "Some of the big dailies will be sending a regular man, though the smaller papers will be relying on their usual correspondents. After all, this is just as big as amateur baseball gets. I imagine this tournament will be pretty well scouted, especially the Class A games."

"Do you know any big league scouts?"

"Not any of the prominent ones, although almost any man interested in baseball might have a loose connection with some professional organization, and pass along occasional tips. Newspaper reporters are the best scouts of all, because they see a good many games in their own territories, and give the best players write-ups. In the case of a local hero, they may even try to interest some big league team. The most important scouts—those employed by major league teams—are in a peculiar position. They would like to remain anonymous to the players so they won't be pestered to death, but on the other hand they have to talk with managers and reporters in order to get a line on the players. Sometimes the manager tells a player that he is being scouted, to make sure the player will be trying his best. On the other hand, he might decide not to tell him, for fear it might make him nervous. One way or another, the word usually manages to get around. Only sometimes the word is wrong. Not everyone who claims to be a scout really is one."

Ted frowned. "I can see why a scout might want to pretend that he really isn't a scout. But why should a man claim to be a scout when he isn't?"

"He could have mixed motives." Ken shrugged. "He simply might like the idea of crashing gates, getting good seats, talking to important people, being admitted into private circles. On the other hand he might have something more profitable in mind."

Ted was beginning to get a message, but it was not quite clear. "Like what?" he demanded.

"Well, Ted, you know people like to bet on sports sometimes. I don't object to small, private wagers, but I think we can and should do something about professional gambling rings and the criminal activities which their income supports."

He said no more about it but got up and sauntered about the office, examining the posters. However, he had set Ted to thinking, which was undoubtedly what he had in mind. Ken's paper and Ted's were in competition in much of their circulation areas, and in a sense they were fierce professional opponents. But they were personal friends and Ted knew that Ken's warning–for that was undoubtedly what it was–was well meant. Whatever private tip or information Ken was acting on was not disclosed, but apparently he took it quite seriously, and felt an obligation to alert Ted to the possibilities he foresaw.

"I guess I'll be wandering off," Ken decided, "but you'll be seeing me around almost any time next week. If this meet is important enough for the big dailies, it ought to be big enough for us little country cousins."

After Ken had left, Ted was alone for only a short time because his friends began to arrive to meet the first busload. The bus apparently arrived right on schedule, for at quarter to five a man came into the office.

"I'm Mr. Ingram of the Eagleville Eaglets," he said to Ted.

Mr. Ingram was shown where to register, listing his own name and those of all his athletes, which took several minutes. Then he received the pack of cards from Margaret, and looked them over.

"So our game is at nine o'clock tomorrow," he observed, "and that's at Westgate Park. I presume there won't be any problem about finding it, but I'd better explain to the boys just where it is."

"On the west edge of town–you can't miss it," Nelson informed him. Then, realizing that some of the boys might become confused as to which direction was west, he added, "The tallest tree in town is just behind the backstop."

"I guess that ought to be clear enough," Mr. Ingram agreed with a smile. "I understand my boys are to be housed in private homes."

"Yes," Ted responded. "They want all the Class F boys at the hotel in order to keep them under close observation. The managers, umpires and other officials, and reporters will also be there, too, so that will give the hotel a full house. The older groups coming by private car will get the motels, and the rest are on the town. In fact I'm getting two of your boys myself— Larry Dodge and Cal Farmington."

"Fine boys, both of them. In fact, I'm sure you won't have any trouble with any of our group. They're not angels, but they're too excited about baseball to think of very much else. Perhaps, Ted, you'd like to come outside and meet Larry and Cal now."

"Sure—or better yet, I could take them home right now. They may be getting hungry, and if not, I am!" he concluded with a laugh.

He had a hurried consultation with the others and found that everything was moving smoothly, so he would not be missed for a while. He then followed Mr. Ingram outside. The manager quickly gave each boy his proper card, and reminded them all of the curfew and the time and place of their starting game.

"Be sure they're not late," said Ted to the manager, but loud enough for the entire group to hear. "Practice has to be over and the game begun promptly at nine, because there are six games scheduled on that one field for the day, so none of them can be allowed to drag. Luckily Classes E and F only play seven innings, so that will speed matters up. Good luck, Mr. Ingram—and players."

"Thanks, Ted, we'll all be there by eight-thirty, and we'll hope the dew is dried off the field."

The Eaglets' manager pointed out Larry and Cal to Ted, and the boys were glad to meet him.

"I hope you don't mind walking," Ted observed. "It's not very far, and if we wait for a ride we'll be late for supper."

His house guests assured him they did not mind walking, and Ted got the idea they did not want to be late for supper, either.

"How are the Eaglets going to make out tomorrow?" asked Ted, as they walked along.

"Oh, we'll win," said Larry in a burst of enthusiasm. "Jan Allaine is a pretty good pitcher. He's won eight games this season."

"How many did you win?" asked Ted curiously.

"Just one. I've pitched mostly in relief. Jan did almost all of the pitching, but once in a while he got tired, especially when we had three games in a week."

"Do you think you'll get in this week?"

"I hope not!" said Larry quickly. "I mean, I'd like to play, but that would mean that our starting pitcher was in trouble, and I wouldn't want that. But I'll be ready if they need me."

"A catcher is almost as important as the pitcher," said Cal, who was a catcher.

"How many games did you play?" asked Ted.

"Oh, one game I played almost the whole game, after Simon, the first-string man, hurt his hand." And so Ted learned that for all their enthusiasm, Larry and Cal had spent most of the season on the bench.

"Are you a newspaper reporter, Ted?" Larry asked him a little later.

"Part time, anyway."

"Did you ever work on any big stories?" asked Cal eagerly.

"Well, there've been a few that we thought were pretty big at the time." At least these boys had come from a town little bigger than Forestdale, and so they were not likely to be critical either of its size or of its newspaper.

They asked for a few details, and Ted supplied them as best he could. But as he finished, Larry had a question.

"Does that mean that we have to be careful about everything we say, because you might quote us in the newspaper?"

Ted smiled. "I don't think it will be that bad. Most of the time I'll be acting as your host. When I start acting like a newspaper reporter, I'll let you know."

"What will we do Tuesday when we don't have a game?" asked Cal. Apparently the thought that the Eaglets might lose their game and be back home by Monday night had not occurred to him.

"Well, on Tuesday Mr. Ingram might be able to arrange a practice for you on the practice field."

"Why don't they use it for regular games?" asked Larry.

"Too narrow, but it'll do for practice. Then, too, you'll get a chance to watch the other teams play. And besides the regular things around the town, there's going to be a model-airplane flying competition lasting most of the week. And you might want to attend Jack Hart's baseball clinic."

"He was a real pitching star, wasn't he?"

"He was pretty good, all right, but chronic shoulder trouble put him out of the major leagues before he could establish himself as one of the top men. Remember how he pitched nineteen consecutive no-hit innings, even though he never got a no-hitter?"

"How did he do that?" asked Cal, puzzled, for Hart had not been a relief pitcher.

"He allowed two hits in the first inning of a game, then pitched no-hit the rest of the way, though the game went through thirteen innings. Then his next game he gave up no-hits until the eighth inning. He lost that one, though."

"Tough luck," was Larry's opinion, and the others had to agree that it was. Hart was a pitcher who was reputed to have had a lot of hard luck during his brief career.

Mrs. Wilford welcomed the boys and heaped up their plates when they joined her and Ted at the table. After supper Ted asked what they would like to do, adding:

"I have to get back to headquarters for a while, but you don't have to come unless you want to."

But they immediately decided they wanted to go with him, though they planned to be back by nine o'clock for a mystery on television. After Ted left the boys to look around town, he found things going less smoothly than before at the office. More teams had arrived, and a few clerical errors had been discovered which had to be corrected. He also found that his staff had made up a list of complaints for him to take care of. Most of these complaints involved mere misunderstandings, which were easily explained. Some complaints were fully justified, and he adjusted them as best he could. The remainder concerned matters he couldn't do anything about–he could only hope to soothe ruffled feelings.

His visitors were home and presumably asleep by the time he arrived, having been the last to leave the office. He turned in promptly himself and fell asleep with little trouble. He would probably have slept undisturbed the night through, had not the telephone in his room begun to ring a short time after midnight. He stumbled over to it in the dark, and offered a sleepy "Hello?"

"Ted? This is Sergeant Jeffers. Someone has broken into baseball headquarters. You'd better come right down and see if anything is missing."

3 An Angry Manager

Entry into the office seemed to have been accomplished in a professional manner. A pane of glass had been removed in the rear door, enabling the intruder to reach in and unfasten the bolt. But what was there in the office to attract a professonal burglar? There was no money or other valuables. All the office contained, besides the baseball records, was a few tables and chairs and some secondhand office machines which were of little value and probably could not be sold anyway. The equipment seemed to have been untouched. A file box full of cards had been overturned on the floor, and the upright file cabinet had been disturbed. One of the drawers was still open, and had obviously been rummaged through.

"What could anyone have wanted in there?" Ted wondered aloud.

"They might have thought you had a few valuables put away for safekeeping," Sergeant Jeffers pointed out. "It's a common practice to turn such things in to headquarters until they are needed."

Ted shook his head. "None of the local people could have thought that. They know Mr. Dobson has a safe in the office next door, and any valuables would have been placed in there. As a matter of fact, that is just what happened."

"Who said anything about *local* people?" the sergeant demanded.

"You think it was some of the visitors?"

"Why not? We've had very little trouble along this line before. Now we're invaded by youthful visitors, and immediately trouble breaks out."

"Maybe because we've never had a baseball headquarters before for anyone to break into," said Ted with a half smile. "What do *you* suppose they were after?"

"Seeing how little of value is here, with no apparent attempt to take even what there was, I would guess that it was just two boys away from home looking for adventure."

"How do you know it was done by boys?"

"I don't even have to guess because Mr. Condon saw them." Mr. Condon ran an office on the other side of the block, the rear of his property touching the rear of the *Town Crier* allotment. "He happened to be out in back with a flashlight checking on his rubbish cans when he thought he noticed a light over here. He flashed his light this way, and that apparently alarmed the boys, for they ran out. He got a pretty good look at them."

"Good enough to identify them?"

"No, but at least he was pretty certain they were boys. And he didn't think they were carrying anything–at least not anything very bulky."

Ted reflected. Mr. Condon was a responsible man. Still, in the dark, it was quite possible that he had made a mistake about their size, especially since he realized the town was full of strange boys anyway. On the other hand it was much more probable that he was correct. But why would two boys want to break into the office? He was not willing to accept Sergeant Jeffers' theory.

Kids out on a lark didn't quite fit the facts. Boys looking for trouble could easily have created havoc in that office in a very few minutes, by dumping out drawers and overturning everything in sight. These intruders had only overturned one small box, and in the dark that could easily have been accidental. But what better theory was there? Ted was unable to come up with anything.

"Do you know of anything that is missing?" the sergeant inquired.

"No, I don't, but the girls will probably be able to tell better in the morning. Is it possible for me to talk with Mr. Condon?"

"Yes, he's outside, speaking to the officer in the police car."

Ted stepped out, and Mr. Condon repeated the story which he had already told to Sergeant Jeffers.

"How tall were these boys?" asked Ted.

Mr. Condon held his hand up to his chin, indicating they were about five feet tall, or a little more. This was not necessarily conclusive, for there are men no taller than that, as Ted reminded him.

"It wasn't only their size," the businessman went on. "They were wearing the jackets that most of the ballplayers wear, and their manner of movement—the way they ran—also suggested that they were boys rather than men."

"Which way did they run?"

"Straight down the alley."

"That would have carried them right into the brightly lighted business district, and the police were on the lookout for boys out after the curfew. They would have done better to turn down the drive, and circle back through the quieter streets."

"I know. Local boys would have known it, unless they were too excited. But visiting boys might not."

Since Mr. Condon was the only witness who had come forward, what could one do but believe him? Still, Ted was disappointed—just as he knew Mr. Dobson would be—that something like this had happened so soon. What would things be like by the end of the week?

He thanked Mr. Condon and returned to the office. Sergeant Jeffers was dutifully dusting the back door and the file cabinet for fingerprints, but without much hope that they could be identified.

"Hardened criminals, yes. Boys, no," he said disgruntledly. "And I thought baseball was supposed to keep boys out of trouble."

Ted shrugged and went on home where he had trouble falling asleep. When he did finally make it, the alarm clock seemed to ring the next minute. Faced with a busy day, he knew that by afternoon he would miss that two or three hours of lost sleep. But there was no help for it; he would have to get up and on his way.

Larry and Cal, having heard his alarm, got up at about the same time and came down for an early breakfast with him. They were already dressed in their baseball uniforms, except for their baseball shoes which they would carry down to the field with them. They seemed a little more subdued as game time loomed closer. Probably neither would get into the game that day, but they seemed as concerned as though the outcome depended entirely upon their efforts. There was some talk about pitching, the caliber of their opponents and the condition of the field, leading Mrs. Wilford, who overheard some of this conversation while she was busy serving breakfast, to suppose they were the stars of the team!

Then it was time for Ted to be off, and he wished them the best of luck as he took his departure.

"Will you be at the game?" asked Larry in parting.

Ted shook his head. "Can't make it on a Monday morning. But I'll have the score by telephone almost as soon as it's over."

The morning was still slightly cool. There was mist in the air, and traces of dew on the grass. But Ted felt, optimistically, that the sun would break through and give them a pleasant and not-too-warm day. This was what the weatherman had promised.

Some of his friends were already waiting at the office, and he found them excited by the news—and evidence—that the place had been entered during the night. The girls checked the files, and said that as far as they knew nothing was missing. If it was, it would have to be something small, like a single letter or file card which was hard to check. The mess was soon cleaned up, and they were back in business.

"But I still wonder what those boys wanted," Margaret speculated.

"And whether they got what they wanted," Ted added.

This was their big morning, with a new flood of visitors signing in. Unfortunately some of the teams not scheduled to arrive until late afternoon or evening came in before noon. There was really no place to put them all until the results of today's games were in and it was known which rooms would be available. Their luggage was shunted to the high-school gym, and they wandered around rather like lost souls.

Ted's plans had been based on the belief that no team would bring more than its proper quota of players, and that some might be a player or two short. Now he learned that the exact opposite was the case. He saw at least two boys with broken arms who had come anyway, and one crippled boy who obviously could not have played on any team, but had come in some capacity with the others. Ted wished them all well, but there just wasn't going to be room for everyone, and he expected that cots would have to be set up in the gym.

Well, Monday night would be the big squeeze, Ted decided. Tuesday night might be almost as bad, but after that enough defeated teams would have departed so there would be no further need for cots in the gym.

Ted could not spend the entire morning at baseball headquarters. The *Town Crier's* deadline was noon, and it was important that the Tuesday morning edition should contain as complete an account of the baseball activity as possible. Ted had his regular story outlined, but had to complete it and type it up for the printer. Then there were the results of the baseball games coming in. At least two games, one on each field, would be completed before noon, and with good luck the second games might also be finished. Sometime in midmorning Ted received a call from Nelson that the Eaglets had won by a score of three to one, and he was happy for Larry and Cal. Nelson told him that the starting battery had completed the game, and gave him the highlights, and Ted realized that neither Larry nor Cal had gotten into the game.

Ted had instructed Nelson, at Westgate, and Jim Wessox, at Eastgate, to call him just before noon, regardless of whether or not the games they were watching at that time were completed. Jim called early, telling him that his game was over, and supplying him with details. But Nelson, who had not been scoring his game but had been taking pictures for a later edition of the *Town Crier*, called at almost the last-possible minute, saying that the game was in the last inning. Since one team held a five-run lead over the other, it would have been tempting to assume the result, but Ted played it cautious, knowing there was still the possibility of an upset. That was all he could do now, and he pounded out the remainder of the story on his typewriter and hurried with it to the printer.

With the deadline met, he breathed a little easier. As always, it seemed to him that the world itself slowed down at noon on Mondays and Thursdays, deadline days. He went home for lunch, where Larry and Cal gave him a full account of the morning's game. Even though they hadn't played, it had been an exciting one for them.

"Now what do you fellows intend to do this afternoon?" asked Ted, for they had nothing on schedule until Wednesday afternoon.

"What choice do we have?" asked Larry.

"There's a Class A game at Eastgate, and another Class E game at Westgate—the winner may meet you in the finals. Or if you have had enough of games for a while, there's Jack Hart's baseball clinic at the practice field, or the model-airplane races in the south meadow."

The two boys looked at each other. All these things were tempting, but they decided that duty required them to watch the Class E game, although they hoped to find time for some of the other things, too.

Depending on how things were running at headquarters, Ted had hopes of watching at least part of a game himself. Class A was the big attraction where he knew most of the out-of-town reporters would be found. But there was even greater local interest in the Forestdale Rangers' Class C game in the evening. This was the only Forestdale team to make the play-offs, and hopes were running high for the local boys. Ted knew a number of the players intimately and felt they had a good chance.

Back at headquarters he found things no more hectic than usual, and so he hurried out to Eastgate.

Ken Kutler was one of the reporters at the game, and he introduced Ted to some of the others. From the conversation he picked up, Ted learned that a number of the players in the game were considered big league material, and were heroes in their home towns. It should have been a good afternoon, but Ted found himself a little uneasy. He didn't want to stay out of touch with his office for too long, and he left before the game was over.

He arrived at headquarters in time to see an obviously angry man involved in some exchange with the girls at the desk. They turned to him in relief as he came in.

"What's the trouble?" he inquired.

The man turned to him. "Are you the one in charge of this rat race?"

"I'm Ted Wilford of the *Town Crier*. Can I help you?"

"Well, I'm Mr. Wyatt of the Stanton Bearcats." Ted mentally placed them as a Class C team. "I just wondered how anyone with a brain in his skull could think that six games could be played on one baseball diamond in one day. Are you the one responsible?"

"I helped draw up the schedule, yes." There seemed no point in mentioning that Mr. Dobson had been chiefly responsible, and Mr. Wyatt must have been aware that the schedule had been approved by the state committee.

"Well, what do you intend to do about my team? We're scheduled for evening—I suppose that means *this* evening, provided none of the other games happen to drag into long extra innings. Well, I don't intend to have my boys playing out there in the dark."

"We figured that there would be time enough," said Ted mildly.

"It's playing it pretty close to the line. What if the sky is overcast? Then it will be too dark even if the game does start on time by some miracle."

"There are lights at Eastgate," Ted reminded him.

"I know, I've been here before, and I've seen your lights. You know they're not good enough for night baseball."

"Possibly not, but they help out at twilight."

"And if we don't get the game in?"

"Then we'll have to move it up to tomorrow."

"That would give us games on Tuesday, Wednesday, and Friday."

"If you win," muttered some unidentified voice in the background, but Mr. Wyatt chose to ignore it.

"Do you think we want to play games on consecutive days?" Mr. Wyatt went on bitterly. "Do you think we're made of pitchers?"

"The teams that win on Thursday will have to play on Friday, too," Ted pointed out. "That was the only way we could arrange the schedule. There are traveling and living costs we have to keep down, too. Most of these teams are short of money, you know."

"Well, all I've got to say is that I think you've done a blamed poor job of arranging. My team won't play if it's too dark, and if you schedule us for Tuesday, the state committee is going to hear from me. And if I have anything to say about it, the games will never come to this one-horse town again."

"And if I have my way, you'll never come back to Forestdale, either," commented Nelson, who had just arrived, but it was not heard by Mr. Wyatt who was already slamming out of the office.

4   Shattered Glass

Ted always tried to decide whether or not a complaint was justified. In this case he felt that it was not. It was true that conditions in Forestdale were a little less than ideal, but all this was anticipated and explained in the plan which Mr. Dobson had submitted and the state committee had approved. Mr. Wyatt had surely seen the plan weeks ago, and should have made any complaints at that time. He must have realized, Ted decided, there was nothing to be done about it now, and had come in just to throw his weight around.

"Kind of an alibi in advance," was Nelson's comment. "Then if something goes wrong, he will have somebody to blame it on. I've heard about the Bearcats. The Stanton paper called them a 'fighting' team, but you can take that two ways. What's a bearcat, anyway? I didn't know there was such an animal."

"I think they mean a panda," said Ted absently, not explaining that he had had occasion to look it up in the dictionary a few weeks before. He looked at his watch. "What are you doing here? Aren't you scoring the next game at Westgate?"

"Yes, but I had to dash back with a message, and if you think it's going to make you feel any better, you're crazy. Jim Wessox passed the word along to me. The lights at Eastgate aren't working!"

"Holy mackerel!" Ted exclaimed with a groan. "What's Jim doing about it?"

"He's got an electrician looking into it, but they're not very hopeful about getting things working by tonight."

"Well, can't something be done to speed things up?"

24

"He could call out a whole crew, I suppose, though they're not sure that would help any. Besides, you know what that would mean. The alarm would be out. And when you're dealing with a man like Mr. Wyatt, you can be certain that the minute he knows something is wrong with the lights he will demand that the lights be turned on immediately. But it's up to you."

It was a difficult decision to make. Ted's natural inclination was to put the electrical crew to work at full speed, and if they failed, at least there would be no reasonable way to blame him. Conversely, this might be a situation where a little bluff, no matter how much he disliked it, would be the best solution. Certainly a protested game, or even a postponed or interrupted game, would upset matters considerably. Wouldn't it be human nature, if a team should find itself a number of runs behind, to stall around hoping that the game would have to be called off because of darkness? So far the games were moving along smoothly and ought to be finished in plenty of time without lights. Even at Westgate, where there were no lights, he was expecting no trouble for a number of shorter Class E and Class F games had been scheduled there.

"We'll bluff it," Ted decided. "Keep the electrician working quietly, and we'll hope he finds the trouble. But don't let on anything's wrong."

"Right! And I'll even forget I told you the lights were out of commission, in case anyone should ask."

"Well . . . let's just say that you won't broadcast it around, in case no one asks. And maybe if we're lucky the Bearcats will lose tonight, and we'll be rid of them and Mr. Wyatt once and for all."

"You'd better hope they win, so that Mr. Wyatt won't have a *real* beef," and Nelson left.

Ted kept busy for a while; the phone kept ringing, visitors kept dropping in. But he was very drowsy after the loss of sleep the night before, and decided he'd better take a walk.

It was still a bright afternoon, without a trace of clouds. He supposed he ought to be getting over to Eastgate to see what was happening with the lights. The Class A game was probably over by now, and most of the reporters would have left, for the Class D game to follow would hold little attraction for them unless one of the teams was from their home town. Still, Ted followed a somewhat roundabout route to take him to the park. He decided to stop off at Forestdale High, where one end of the football field, behind the end zone, had been turned into a practice diamond.

There, as expected, he found Jack Hart busy with his baseball clinic. A crowd of interested boys were gathered around him, among them Larry and Cal. Jack was demonstrating proper grip on the ball and proper pitching motion, and would occasionally let the ball fly at an older boy standing before the backstop. Ted did not approach closely enough to hear what was said, but he knew that Jack was capable of holding their attention for a long time. As a recent major league star, his achievements were still remembered by his young fans. He had a number of gadgets to show, too, including a mechanical pitcher, and an electronic home plate which called balls and strikes. Of course there was no chance of his selling any of these devices to his young audience, but the manufacturer had hired him to demonstrate them wherever he had a suitable chance.

Jack happened to look up and caught Ted's eye. "Hi, there, Wilford," he called. "Going to join us?"

"Haven't time now," Ted replied with a friendly wave of his hand, and strolled on. He had not met Jack Hart before, and wondered how the pitcher happened to know his name. He might have heard of Ted as the person in charge of baseball headquarters, but would not have recognized him unless someone had pointed him out. It could have been one of the boys in the group, possibly Larry or Cal, though none of them had appeared to notice Ted's approach.

As Ted was walking through the outskirts of the business section, the loud crash of shattered glass startled him. He spun about in time to see three boys dashing out of a cross street and running off in the opposite direction from him. They took another turn at the next block, and were out of sight before he could chase them. Though I don't think I would have had much chance of catching them anyway, the way they were going, he justified his failure to get started.

It was then that he heard a loud alarm bell, though it must have been ringing before he noticed it. He walked back to the corner and down the street from which the boys had fled. He saw at once that a little crowd had gathered around a jewelry-store window, while the burglar alarm was clanging madly. The plate-glass window had a small hole in it, and several long cracks, and this had touched off the alarm.

The proprietor had come out and was examining the window to make sure that no one had reached inside and—at the risk of cutting his arm severely—helped himself to some of the expensive jewelry. This was undoubtedly the reason he had not set off in pursuit of the boys himself. Having reassured himself that nothing was missing so far, he turned to face the crowd.

"Did anybody see which way they went?"

As no one answered, Ted volunteered, "I saw them turn into Malcolm Avenue, but I don't think there's any chance of catching them now. They've probably separated and mingled with the other boys."

That burglar alarm would probably bring the police in short order, and much as he would have liked to leave, Ted realized that he was a witness and was obliged to stay. He hoped that at least Sergeant Jeffers would not be in the police car, but this was not his lucky day! Jeffers was soon there, looking grim.

The proprietor quickly explained matters to Jeffers. "I happened to notice these boys hanging around outside, but I didn't think much about it. It was broad daylight after all, and lots of people like to stop and admire my jewelry. Well, something called me into the back of the store, and that must have been just what they were waiting for. I heard the crash of glass and the alarm went off. That must have scared them, and they took off without trying to grab anything."

"Did you see what they threw at the window? Was it a baseball?"

"I don't think they threw anything. They must have been holding rocks in their hands, and pounded at the glass."

"Or it might have been baseballs–hard balls?" asked the sergeant, with a side glance at Ted.

"Well, maybe. I didn't think about that."

"You were lucky nothing was taken." Jeffers was looking over the price tags. "You have some pretty expensive merchandise here."

The jeweler looked embarrassed. "Maybe you'd better not believe every sign you see. If people come in, we don't cheat them. But in the window–maybe yes. They can't tell from a distance whether it's real or paste, and we don't particularly want to expose our best stuff to vandals."

"I understand, but that's neither here nor there. These boys undoubtedly *thought* that the stuff was expensive. I don't suppose you recognized them?"

"No, but I didn't get a very good look at them. Ted, here, may have seen them better than I did."

"But they could have been ballplayers?"

"They could have been. I just don't know."

The officer turned to Ted. "Did you get a good look at them?"

"Not very. They were running in the opposite direction from me."

"Then you couldn't have recognized them?"

"No."

"Not even well enough to tell whether they were Forestdale boys or strangers?"

"No, I couldn't even tell that much. All I know for sure is that I saw three of them. They must have been the same boys Mr. Williams says he saw, though I didn't see them break the window."

"How about their ages? What class would they play in?"

"They would be Class F, probably–if they were ballplayers."

"Are there any Class F games on right now? That might eliminate some of the possibilities."

Ted shook his head. "No Class F games now."

As the officer turned away to talk to some of the other people, Ted decided this would be a good time to leave. Everything Jeffers had said last night now seemed to take on added force, and Ted felt a little sick about it himself. If baseball couldn't help stop delinquency, what could?

At Eastgate Ted located Jim Wessox, who explained a little more clearly the nature of the trouble there.

"Any chance of hurrying things along?" asked Ted.

"Do you want ladders all over the place, and wires stretched along the field?"

"No, I guess not." Ted saw that that wouldn't do at all. There was a Class D game in progress and it meant a good deal to these players. There was no point in getting panicky over the lights not working just because Mr. Wyatt was a disagreeable man.

As long as he was there Ted thought it a good idea to watch part of the game. The Class A boys would be getting plenty of publicity. Why not give some of it to the Class D boys, too, if they showed they deserved it? With this in mind, he talked with the official scorer, covering the part of the game he had missed, and made a few notes. Then he settled back to watch a few innings of the game. He saw some surprisingly good plays, and jotted down the names of the players concerned. He didn't believe there was anyone there the professional scouts would be interested in, but in a year or two who could say?

He finally left, reluctantly, for the game was a close one but time was running out if he were to stop back at the office and then get home in time for supper. At headquarters he found nothing more doing than anticipated. No more check-ins or check-outs were expected for the rest of the day, and the staff could afford to draw a few extra breaths. They were now acting as an information booth, and one person could handle most of the work. But beginning tomorrow, they would start to get the reports of the official scorers, and those calculating machines would begin clicking. They would have to compile a box score for each individual game, recording all the required information and mimeographing sufficient copies. Then there were the individual record cards for each player. Cards for teams eliminated from the tournament could soon be completed but they would have to wait for all the others. It would take several days after the tournament was over to complete all this work and get the records into the proper hands.

While Ted was there a call came in inquiring whether the Bearcats' game would be allowed to continue under the lights, if it ran long enough. Ted replied that that had been the original understanding, but he kept his fingers crossed as he spoke.

He made it home in time for supper. Cal and Larry were there, too, but Ted found it difficult to keep his mind on the younger boys' chatter and plans for the future, and suppressed several yawns. He decided to take a little nap. The office knew where to reach him if anything important came up.

"Call me in fifteen minutes, will you, Mom?" he asked.

His mother promised that she would, and very nearly did, for it was about twenty minutes later that she aroused him from his nap. He took a quick shower, changed clothes, and was ready to go out.

"What are you boys doing this evening?" he inquired of his visitors.

"What games are playing?" asked Cal.

"Class C at both fields. The Stanton Bearcats are playing at Eastgate, and they're favored to win in their class. But we haven't given up on the Forestdale Rangers, playing at West-gate."

"Are you going to Westgate, Ted?" Larry questioned.

Ted shook his head. If there was going to be trouble with Mr. Wyatt at Eastgate, that was where he belonged. Both he and Nelson would have liked to watch the Rangers, having friends on the team. But Nelson was scheduled to act as scorer for the Bearcats' game—the third game he had scored that day. There would be three more tomorrow, but after that this chore would be ended for him.

"Then we'll go to Westgate and watch the game for you so we can tell you what happened," Larry decided suddenly.

As Ted was about to leave, the telephone rang. It was Cliff Corby down at the gym.

"Ted, they want to move about thirty cots into the gym tonight. They may not need them all, but they want to be sure to have enough. So I'm going to need some help. Whom can you get?"

"Whom can I get? Don't you know the Rangers are playing tonight? Almost everybody we know will be down there. I don't dare ask them."

"Well, it wouldn't take so *awfully* long if we had enough help. What about Nel and Jim?"

"Nel's scoring the Bearcats, so he doesn't dare be late. And Jim's doing—other things." Ted remembered that he would probably still be working with the electrician.

"Well, I can't do it all myself," Cliff complained. "With about fifty million boys in town, there ought to be a few extra muscles available."

"I'll have to come down myself, Cliff, and I'll pick up any-body I can get hold of along the way."

The boys had overheard part of this conversation and eagerly volunteered their services.

"And then we'll get over to Westgate and report the game for you," said Larry happily.

5   High, Inside

Ted and the boys stopped in at headquarters but found nothing there to detain them. Then they went on to the gym where they found Cliff alone and overwhelmed, though he was doing his best. His face lit up when he saw the three boys.

"I couldn't be happier if you were the United States Marines," he exclaimed. "Did you ever try lifting one of these cots alone?"

"You shouldn't have tried," Ted said. "I told you I'd be coming along."

"Well, I knew you'd try, but I figured there might be dozens of people who would buttonhole you along the way. Shall we get with it, gentlemen?"

The boys proved to be willing workers, and it did not take very long to bring some order to the gym.

"That'll do," Cliff finally ordered. "I can handle the rest of it myself."

"Aren't you going to try to get to the Rangers' game?" Ted inquired.

"I'd like to, but I never know when I'll begin to get some customers, and I've got too much to do. This is the life," and he flung himself down on one of the cots and pretended to fall asleep.

Outside, Ted and the boys separated, the Eaglets hurrying off toward Westgate, and Ted heading eastward. It was still a bright evening, with the sun a considerable distance above the horizon. If the game didn't run too long, everything was going to be all right. Arriving at the field, he discovered it was the top of the third inning. That wasn't as far along as he had hoped, but there was still time. Only then did he look at the scoreboard to learn that the Bearcats were leading the Lakeland Bombardiers by five to one.

There was only a small crowd here, and he had no trouble locating Nelson and finding a seat next to him. He made a significant gesture toward the lights, and Nelson shook his head.

"Nothing doing there, Ted. Just keep your fingers crossed."

"It isn't too bad for now," Ted observed.

"No, and if the Bearcats keep their lead, they won't have to play the last half of the ninth inning, so that will save some time. But you've missed most of the fun, Ted. That Bearcat pitcher is wild, high and inside."

"Deliberate?"

Nelson shrugged. "You're entitled to your opinion, and I'm entitled to mine. But mine is that it couldn't be anything *but* deliberate. Every time he gets into a jam, he reaches back into his bag of tricks and comes up with a bean ball."

"The umpires doing anything?"

"Not so far. If you asked them, they'd say they're not mind readers. And how do I know what they'd say? Because I'm a mind reader."

Ted knew that throwing bean balls was not uncommon in the big leagues, but he hated to see it on the amateur level. It was true that the players were wearing helmets, and these pitchers were not as fast as older players. But the lighting was not too good, and the boys had had less experience in dodging the ball, so someone might get hurt.

"What do you think about the bean ball, Nel?"

"I know that some big league pitchers say they need it to keep the batters from digging in and teeing off on the ball, though it's my opinion they're afraid of the batters. They distinguish between really trying to hit the batter—in which case they aim at the middle of the back because that's the hardest pitch to duck away from—and brushing him back, or making him eat dust. But that's like calling the same thing by different names, because how can they be sure the batter will get out of the way? Some batters even approve of it—especially when their own pitchers are doing it. The umpires don't do much to stop it, and the owners and managers seldom step in."

"Could they do anything about it even if they wanted to?"

"Oh, it wouldn't be much of a problem to stop it. I've heard it suggested that just a little change in the rules would do it. Suppose the ball comes at the batter, but he ducks out of the way. Give him his base just the same as though he'd been hit."

"That's guessing, isn't it?"

"Isn't an umpire guessing anyway? Do you think he's right on every ball and strike, on every close decision? Can he tell if the batter pulled back on his swing or not, when the catcher jumps up in his way? Most times when a batter gets hit by a pitched ball he shrugs it off and trots down to first, but when he knows he has to convince the umpire he's been hit, he goes into a great big act, and then the umpire has to be a mind reader."

Ted grinned. "But you don't think the big leagues are likely to make the change, do you?"

"Oh, I wouldn't try to tell them how to run their business. But I think I could do a good job of telling them what the kids are thinking. Boys make all sorts of explanations and excuses, but they really don't admire players like that. And when they stop admiring players, they'll stop saving up their money for ball tickets and think of something else to do with it."

"And meanwhile we're stuck with kids who are trying to imitate the big leaguers under very different playing conditions."

"That's about it," Nelson agreed. "Our pitchers don't have the speed, but they don't have the control either. Half the time they don't know where the pitch is going themselves."

"This Bearcat pitcher looks like he has pretty good control," Ted observed.

"You bet he has. That's what makes me so sure that he knows exactly what he's doing when he fires that fast one high and inside. He's acting under orders directly from Mr. Wyatt."

"You think so?"

"Let's put it this way—Mr. Wyatt could stop it in a minute if he wanted to."

The side had been retired as they were talking, and Nelson made some further notes on his scoring pad. Then the first Bearcat batter of the inning hit a hard grounder down to shortstop, which the fielder fumbled.

"Hit or error?" Ted questioned.

"Error. He should have had it. I've seen a lot better plays made than that one in Class C. Now if it was Class F I'd call it a hit."

"Aren't they playing under the same rules?" asked Ted with a smile.

"Sure, but the players are about a foot shorter."

A little later Larry Dodge arrived at the field, spotted them in the stands, and came running up to them. He started to speak but Nelson interrupted:

"Save it, kid, till you get your breath. You think this is the marathon? Too bad we don't have radio communication with the other field. It would save wear and tear."

In a few moments Larry had recovered, and addressed Ted. "I just wanted to tell you that the Rangers are ahead, three to nothing, at the end of the fifth inning."

"Good," Ted exclaimed, "but why didn't you wait for the end?"

"I thought you'd want to know. And Cal is waiting till the game's over so he'll be able to give you the rest of it. We got all three runs on a home run by the first baseman."

"Hank Ewer," Nelson recollected. "He'll have something to

tell his brother Fred now. Fred Ewer," he went on to explain to Larry, "plays in Class A, and is about the best player in town. But Hank's team got into the play-offs, and Fred's didn't."

"Maybe Fred was at the game," Ted suggested.

"I don't think so. He's driving a truck this summer and he's out of town on a long run. He expects to be back in time for Wednesday's game, though—if the Rangers can hold that lead."

"Is Mr. Dobson a kind of tall, gray-haired, distinguished-looking man?" Larry asked Ted.

"That seems to describe Mr. Dobson pretty well. Why?"

"He was over at Westgate. He arrived just a little while after I got there, and everybody stood up and applauded him. The stands were filled already, but they found a seat for him in the best section. For a minute I thought it was the mayor."

"They must be grateful to him for bringing the games here," Ted remarked, and hoped that the trouble with the lights wasn't going to change anybody's mind about that. If Larry had left at the end of the fifth inning, they were probably in the seventh inning by now, and the game was nearly over. They were probably all right at Westgate, barring a tie score and extra innings. Ted wished things had moved along as fast here, for the sun was dropping ever closer to the horizon.

"I don't think they're going to be too anxious to turn on the lights," said Nelson, reading his thoughts. "The Bearcat pitcher is a little faster, and I don't think Mr. Wyatt would be willing to give up the advantage they get by pitching in the twilight."

"What about the Bombardiers' manager?"

"Maybe he doesn't think it makes any difference, or maybe he's a better sportsman than Mr. Wyatt. If it's left up to the umpires, I'm pretty sure they'll try to finish the game by daylight if they can. Some people don't like a mixture of daylight and artificial light—they say it clashes and they can't see as well. And it's hard on the fielders. Just now they have to worry about not looking straight into the setting sun. With the lights on, they have to worry about not looking straight into a bank of lights. And if the lights are turned on too early, they may have to worry about both things."

"I wish it would go on into dark," said Larry enthusiastically. "I'd like to see a game under the lights." Ted and Nelson did not tell him that he wasn't going to see a game under the lights *that* particular night.

During the top of the sixth inning, Ted had a chance to see what Nelson meant. The Bearcat pitcher found himself in trouble with two runners on. Ted did not know the name of the next batter, but saw from Nelson's scorecard that he was batting in fourth position, and so was probably one of their best hitters. That seemed to be all the incentive the pitcher needed to send him sprawling in the dirt, luckily avoiding the fast ball which had been coming straight at his head. The batter got up, dusted himself off, and without a word stepped back into the box. He hit the next pitch for a long fly, which scored a run. Then the attack fizzled, and his team did not score again that inning.

"That batter tripled off him before, and the pitcher remembers," Nelson pointed out. "Do you believe me now?"

"Oh, I believed you before," said Ted quickly, "but seeing is better."

"That was a bean ball, wasn't it?" asked Larry.

"What do you think?"

"Sure looked like it."

"What would you do if the other pitcher was throwing bean balls?" Ted inquired.

"Why, I'd throw bean balls back at them until they stopped. That's what the big leaguers do."

"And what would your manager have to say about that?"

Larry looked thoughtful, and a little uncertain. "I know Mr. Ingram wouldn't tell us to do a thing like that. But I'm not sure he would make us stop if the other team started it."

With a momentary lull in the proceedings in the eighth inning, Ted recalled that he had not yet told Nelson about the jewelry-store window, and he now supplied him with the details.

"Good gravy," Nelson exclaimed, "that's worse than breaking into the office last night. Do you think it was the same boys?"

"I don't know. There's no way to prove it, though there seemed to be only two last night and three today. They appear to have been after two entirely different things. But what makes you think the jewelry-store business is worse?"

"Well, isn't it? Jewelry is valuable, and there wasn't anything of value in the office."

"But at least the jewelry affair took place in broad daylight, while the other was a sneaky type of entry, and we don't know what they were after."

"Somebody broke into your newspaper office last night?" asked Larry.

"No, the baseball headquarters."

"What do you suppose they wanted there?" Larry inquired.

"I can't think of anything at all, unless they just wanted to look over our records."

"Shucks, we would have showed them if they'd asked us," Nelson observed.

"I know, but maybe they didn't realize that, or were afraid to ask for some reason," Ted answered.

"What sort of records do you have there?" asked Larry curiously.

"Nothing very important—mostly correspondence."

"And the results of last year's play-off games," Nelson added.

"Would those be valuable, Ted—like maybe to a scout?" wondered Larry.

"A scout would probably have all that information, and if not he could ask us for it. We'd keep his inquiry confidential if he wanted us to."

"Oh." Larry subsided for the moment, and if he had any

further questions he was prevented from asking them by the arrival of Ken Kutler.

"Game's over," he announced to the others. "Forestdale took it, three to one."

"Yippee!" was Nelson's reaction, expressed for them all.

But they had their own game to consider, too. There was no more bean-balling. The Bombardier pitcher was having so much trouble with his control that he could not afford to waste a pitch, and the Bearcat hurler was not in a jam. Still the Bombardiers, though obviously the weaker team, were hanging in there gamely, but were unable to whittle down the Bearcats' lead.

By the middle of the eighth inning, the sun was touching the distant hilltops and there was a definite haze across the field. Under ordinary conditions the umpires would probably have called for the lights, but with the game so nearly over, they seemed to have decided to keep on as they were.

Though Ted would have liked to see the Bombardiers win, if they were going to lose he hoped they would do so without further scoring by either side, which might prolong the game. And in this, at least, he had his wish. The three batters coming up for the Bombardiers in the top of the ninth all hit the ball, but each time it went directly toward a fielder and became an out. The game was over.

"Whee! That was close," said Nelson in relief, though no one except Ted understood what he meant.

Although the Bearcats were jubilant over their victory, Mr. Wyatt soon broke away from the group and came over to the stands.

"What did you give our batter on that grounder in the third inning?" he inquired of Nelson.

"It was an error on the shortstop."

"What do you mean? That was a clear hit. Anybody could see that. You must have been prejudiced against our team."

Nelson exchanged glances with Ted. If they were prejudiced

against the Bearcats, it was only because Mr. Wyatt had made them prejudiced. The Bearcats had won the game. What more did he want? They could hardly avoid the feeling that all he wanted was to argue.

"Anyway, I'm glad we didn't have to finish under the lights," the manager went on. "They don't look as though they would have helped much!" Ted and Nelson didn't dare to look at each other.

Then Mr. Wyatt turned to Ted. "Seriously, Wilford, if Forestdale wants these games again, they ought to build another diamond–and at least put an addition on that country hotel. As a matter of fact, I don't know why the games should be held in just one town. Each class could be held in a different place."

Ken supported the Forestdale tournament, however, by pointing out:

"I can see where there'd be a lot of saving this way–having one clerical staff, rotating umpires and official scorers, doubling up on housing."

"Money isn't everything," said Mr. Wyatt stiffly.

He stalked off, and they saw him drive away in his green convertible, several of his players accompanying him.

Then Cal Farmington chugged up, apparently having trotted all the way from Westgate to bring them the final score. They did not have the heart to tell him they had already heard it from Ken.

"Want to meet me at the hotel tomorrow morning at nine?" Ken asked Ted. "There are a few people there I want you to meet."

"OK," Ted agreed wonderingly, knowing there was something more to this than Ken was letting on. If it was a newspaper story, why was he taking Ted along, and if it wasn't a story, why was Ken interested?

Then the four boys piled into Nelson's car and started for home.

❂

6   Three Scouts

At nine o'clock the next morning, Ted and Nelson drew into the hotel's parking lot.

"Coming in?" Ted queried, stepping out of the car.

"Not me. I wasn't invited. I'll wait here."

"You don't have to wait if you don't want to. I don't know how long I'll be. When are you due at Westgate?"

"Not till ten-thirty. I'll wait as long as I can, and work on some of my figures in the car. What do you think Ken Kutler is up to, anyway?"

"Hanged if I know. Knowing him, I imagine he's following up a story of some sort. If he is, he won't tell me any more than he wants to, and I can't ask. But why he wants me here I can't imagine."

Ted inquired at the desk, and was told to go up to room 306. He walked up the two flights, and knocked on the proper door, which was opened at once by Ken Kutler. Ted saw that there were three men seated in the room, and Ken introduced them.

"Ted, I want you to meet three men who are more than a little interested in amateur baseball. As a matter of fact they are baseball scouts. This is Mr. Hill . . . and Mr. Saunders . . . and Mr. Scotch."

Ted acknowledged the introductions and waited to hear what the meeting was all about.

"I suppose you're wondering about this, Ted," Mr. Hill began. "You've probably heard that scouting is a cutthroat business. Well, it is. And the reason the three of us are here together is the same reason you and Mr. Kutler are, perhaps, often together. There are times when you'd rather keep your eye on what the opposition is doing. Right, boys?" he asked with a little chuckle, and the other two scouts quickly agreed with him. "Since we all know we're after the same thing, we decided it would be easier if we asked our questions all together, instead of each of us doing it piecemeal."

"What teams are you representing?" asked Ted, as there was a little pause.

"Well, now, that's a slightly embarrassing question. I do have a contract with a minor league team, and they have an arrangement with a major league team, but it's all full of if's, and's, and but's, and any player I signed might end up with an entirely different major league team."

"I represent several minor league teams," Mr. Saunders spoke up. "I know what they need, and I try to get it for them."

Mr. Scotch had nothing to offer.

Ted realized that there was a good deal more here than met the eye. In spite of what they said, he felt sure that these men were actually acting on behalf of major league teams, even if only indirectly. Possibly they felt it wasn't wise to show too much interest in a player for fear he would raise his price. But which player were they after? Then it suddenly clicked, and he knew why Ken had asked him to come. They were after Fred Ewer, and they wanted to get all the information they could about him from Ted before making an approach.

"Of course I know Fred Ewer," said Ted quickly, "but I haven't followed amateur baseball very closely this summer. A friend of mine who is waiting down in the car is much more familiar with the situation than I am. May I bring him up?"

Mr. Hill looked disgruntled. Of course this conference could not have proceeded very far without bringing up Fred's name, but evidently he had hoped to introduce it in his own time and fashion.

"All right, Ted, bring him up," said Mr. Hill at nods from the other two scouts.

Mr. Hill was the most outgoing and quite talkative, Ted decided as he walked down to the car. Mr. Saunders would probably listen with intelligent interest to whatever was going on, and contribute his share when appropriate. Mr. Scotch was a neat, quiet man who sat back and so far had said nothing. The telephone had rung as Ted was leaving, and it was Mr. Scotch who answered, so this was probably his suite of rooms.

Ted soon returned with Nelson, who was introduced to the scouts. He sat down, ready to answer the questions they had for him. But at first their questions seemed somewhat ambiguous and irrelevant.

"What kind of amateur baseball set-up do you have here?" asked Mr. Hill. "That is—" he added, seeing that Nelson did not quite understand "—how many teams do you have in Forestdale?"

"We have one each in Classes A, B, C, and D, two in Class E, and about four in Class F."

"About?"

"Some of the teams disbanded early in the season and were reorganized. The youngest boys start out with enthusiasm, but very often something happens and they drop out."

"Then the upper classes, at least, play entirely with out-of-town teams. How is the competition?"

"It seems pretty good to me. We have had some intersectional games with Stanton and other large places, and we've managed to hold our own."

"But your Class A team didn't make the play-offs."

"No. Fred Ewer had a good year, but some of the other players weren't pulling their weight."

Mr. Hill looked pained, as though he didn't like anyone else to mention Fred.

"About this—ah—Fred Ewer," he brought himself to say, "does he like to hit the fast ball or the curve?"

"Oh, he'll hit anything. But of course he isn't likely to see too many good curves in his class. The pitchers are more likely to rely on a fast ball, and some of them can make it hum."

"Do they always shade him around to right, or does he hit to all fields?" This was the first question from the taciturn Mr. Scotch.

Nelson turned to him, looking a little puzzled. "He's a pretty good pull hitter, but he can hit to all fields. He must have been facing a right-handed pitcher the day you saw him."

Other questions quickly followed. Ted had the feeling that these men were not relying on Nelson's information but were simply using him to verify information that was already in their possession.

"He's been playing the infield," Mr. Saunders pointed out. "Do you think he might do better in the outfield?"

"He might," Nelson conceded. "He's fast, and he has a good peg."

"But in the infield he's kind of a butcher?"

"I wouldn't say that," Nelson objected quickly. "He's not particularly graceful, but he'll go after everything down his way, and come up with most of them."

The scouts looked at each other. Apparently no one had anything further to ask, and Mr. Hill stood up.

"Well, it was nice meeting you gentlemen, and thank you for your help. It's too bad we couldn't have seen this young Ewer in the play-offs, but I did see his brother last night. He might have a future, but of course he's still in high school. I don't know whether it's worth my while to look into this Fred a little more or not. I'll have to consult my principal."

No one else offered anything other than a general good-bye, and the three visitors were shown out into the hall.

"Well, that's that," Nelson complained. "The minute they're finished with us, out we go. I wish *I* could ever get that important. You think they'll do anything about Fred?"

"Whatever they do they'll do fast," Ken assured him. "The baseball season's over as far as Fred's concerned, so there's no use waiting any longer. But you can be pretty sure they won't even tell each other what they're planning to do."

"And meanwhile we don't say anything to Fred about it, right?" asked Ted.

"That would seem to be the best way, Ted. There's no use getting his hopes built up. After all, these scouts may be looking into a lot of players, and of all those they're interested in, they'll sign only a very few."

After Ken had driven off, Nelson said, "Where do you want to go now, Ted? I've got a little time. What are the twins doing today?"

This was his name for Ted's two house guests. "They said something about stopping off for the model-airplane races. Want to give it a look?"

"I sure do," said Nelson enthusiastically. "But can you spare the time?"

"I can if nobody catches me. Then I'll get back to headquarters, and home for lunch, and I have an interview set up with Jack Hart for one o'clock. After all, I'm a newspaper reporter. You want to sit in on that?"

"Jack Hart! I wouldn't miss it for anything," Nelson agreed. "Say, how'd you make out with the lights?"

"Oh, they're working again. The electricians got to work as soon as the field was cleared after the game and put everything to rights."

"And Mr. Wyatt still doesn't know?"

"I don't care what he knows—now that it's all over."

There was quite a crowd gathered in the meadow south of town where the model-airplane competition was being staged. Ted and Nelson got out of the car and began to mingle with the crowd where they soon became aware of their abysmal ignorance. Many of the boys were talking learnedly about airplane construction and design, the problems of flying, and other things which Ted and Nelson found completely over their heads. It was a new field for them, but they were fascinated. They looked over many of the models on display, and were amazed at their resemblance to real planes and by all the detail which could be worked into such a small object.

"Wow! You could sink a fortune into a hobby like this," Nelson decided. "But I could think of worse things to do with it."

They began to pick up some of the rules of the competition and the terminology, and if they had had time enough, might have become real fans. As it was, they felt obliged to leave sooner than they would have liked.

"Just this last event," Nelson suggested, and Ted agreed.

Some young man they did not know was putting his plane through its paces. It moved in a wide circle about him, restrained and controlled by a wire which he held. Suddenly the wire broke or became disconnected, and the plane flew off at a tangent, covering a considerable distance before it finally landed near the edge of the field. No one was standing on that portion of the meadow, but suddenly a boy emerged from the woods. He spotted the plane, ran to it, picked it up, examined it, and looked around. Then he ran back with it into the woods.

"Hey, what's going on?" Nelson exclaimed.

"It looks like he's stealing it," said Ted. The rest of the crowd, too, was looking on in surprise and wonder, too shocked to do anything about it.

"Come on, let's go," Nelson urged Ted.

"Go where?"

"After him, of course. He can't get very far in the woods, even if he has got a good start."

"How could you know him when you found him? He'd probably hide the plane somewhere, and then pretend he was one of the searchers."

"That's right." Nelson stopped in his tracks. "He looked around first to make sure no one was close enough to recognize him, and then he took off. How old would you say he was —thirteen or fourteen?"

"Somewhere around that. It was hard to tell. But I've got a pretty good idea what Sergeant Jeffers is going to say when he hears about it, and I'm not going to like it. He'll be positive it was a ballplayer."

"Well, don't you think it was, Ted? I doubt it was one of the Forestdale boys, because he would be too afraid of being recognized even from this distance. And almost all the visiting boys of that age are ballplayers."

"I guess so," agreed Ted. "I wonder if it could be the same one who was involved in the other things, too? But once it was two of them, and once it was three, and this time it was just one boy. Maybe none of it is connected, and you just have to figure that a certain percentage of boys in a group are going to run hog-wild whenever they get a chance."

"You don't sound very much like Mr. Dobson now."

"No, and maybe I'll end up quitting the newspaper and applying for a job with the police force."

"You sure the theft of the plane will be reported, Ted?"

"There isn't much doubt about it, if they're as valuable as they look."

On the way back to the office, Ted and Nelson saw a police car heading out toward the meadow, and they had no doubt why.

"I kind of wish they would catch that kid," Nelson decided. "Not that I think he is a hardened criminal, or anything like that, but if he finds he can get away with it he may keep right on going."

Then, as if things were not already difficult enough, Ted found Mr. Wyatt just emerging from the office. Ted nodded, and would have liked to pass in, but the manager barred his way.

"Just a minute there, Wilford. I was looking for you. How did it happen that our Bearcats drew two tough opponents for their first two games, and the Forestdale team drew two easy ones? I think our team's good enough to sweep to the championship regardless, but this certainly looks like rank favoritism to me. I wanted to mention this to you yesterday, but didn't have a chance." He made it sound as though Ted had gone slamming out of the office, instead of himself.

"All District One teams were matched with District Two teams in the first round, and the winner meets the winner of the District Three and Four game. It's the same way in each of the classes."

"That may well be, but you'll certainly agree that it favors your hometown team."

"At the time the schedules were drawn up," Ted pointed out, "we had no idea which would be the best teams in each of the divisions. This was the simplest way to arrange the traveling and housing."

"It may have been the simplest, but that doesn't mean it's the best. A fairer way would have been to draw lots to match up the opponents. Then at least we would have known that no one had it in for us."

It seemed useless to argue with the man, so he finally escaped from Mr. Wyatt, who drove off in a two-tone brown sports car. Ted gave a sigh of relief but when he finally entered the office, he found enough headaches awaiting him to challenge an aspirin bottle.

7   Nelson Goes to Bat

Ted had made all possible preparations for his interview with Jack Hart. With the help of newspaper files, the public library and talks with some sports-minded individuals, he had found out all he could about the former pitcher. He had the main details of his career up to the major leagues, and some of the features of his relatively brief service there.

Once an extremely promising young pitcher, Hart had never quite fulfilled that promise. Arm and shoulder trouble had plagued him almost every season, and this, along with the fact that he was playing with a second-division team, had prevented him from achieving the records he might otherwise have made. Twice he had been selected for the all-star squad although he failed to get into the games. Just the year before he had survived spring training and opened the season, only to be cut from the squad when the time approached to reduce the playing roster. No other team had picked up his contract, and so, still less than thirty years old, he found himself out of a job.

But Hart's interest in baseball had not flagged, and though there was no position open for him in the big leagues, he had acquired the sponsorship of a sporting-goods manufacturer, and traveled as a kind of one-man baseball clinic. This job kept him in contact with young players all over the country, which was perhaps the thing he liked best about it. Almost anyone could have demonstrated the manufacturer's equipment, but Hart had the confidence of the boys he met, and could entertain them with a fund of anecdotes or help them with advice based upon his own personal experiences. If Hart quietly and unobtrusively helped an athlete point toward the major leagues, he never made a big production out of it. And if he occasionally dropped a hint to a big league scout that he had discovered a player worth looking at, that was all right. Whether he was paid for any of these tips, Ted did not know, nor did he consider that it was any of his business.

"I suppose you'd like me to keep my big mouth shut at this interview," said Nelson as they drew into the hotel's parking lot for the second time that day.

"Nothing of the sort. Speak right up whenever you want to. You're even more interested in baseball than I am."

Hart was waiting for them, and admitted them to his room. His manner was casual and friendly, the way it had been at the practice field. Ted introduced Nelson to him, but Hart obviously already knew who he was.

"You're one of the official scorers, aren't you?" he asked, as he shook hands.

"That's right," Nelson agreed. Apparently Hart kept his eyes wide open to what was going on around him.

Knowing time was short for all of them, Ted got right down to business. He asked for further details about Hart's career, filling in the smaller points of the outline he had already acquired. Then he went on:

"What advice would you give a young player, Mr. Hart? Just what does it take to make a big league player?"

"The most obvious requirement is the physical equipment. The boy who doesn't have it will, I suppose, have to aspire to nothing more than being a space scientist," he said with a laugh. "But a boy might easily misjudge his physical qualities, and just because he may be slower developing than his friends the same age, he shouldn't become discouraged—he may end up better than they will. Then, too, it is important that he learn to make the best possible use of his physique. I suppose the next most important thing he needs is enthusiasm, and the third is the willingness to work hard. Mental alertness is certainly an important factor, and so, I suppose, is the temperament suited to the pace and climate of the game. You sometimes wonder when you see a big, powerful man sitting over a chessboard why he chose that game, but apparently chess gives him the degree of concentration and tension which is suited to him."

"Then would you recommend a professional career to a young player?"

"I wouldn't recommend anything to anybody. I think he has to decide for himself if that is the sort of life he wants. He must realize that there is always the possibility he won't make the big time. And even if he earns fifty thousand a year, there will be days when his bat and his glove seem to have holes in them. If a batting slump is going to send him into the sulks, or the booing of the crowd get him down, then he'd better take up something else."

"Were you ever troubled much by booing?"

"Oh, I think I received a little more than my share. I won't say it doesn't hurt, but at the same time I didn't blame the crowd, either. They knew what they paid their money to see, and they were letting me know that I wasn't delivering it."

"Unless they paid their money because they wanted the chance to boo somebody," Nelson suggested.

"Well, yes, you run into a few of those in every crowd."

"Did you leave the big leagues on good terms?" Ted continued.

"I think so. I felt that if the manager had let me pitch every fourth day, I would have been able to work out of my troubles. But I can understand why he wouldn't want to let me spot the other team five or six runs a game while I was trying to find myself."

"Couldn't you have worked out your troubles in the bullpen?"

"Believe me, Ted, there's a world of difference between

pitching to an empty plate and pitching to a batter poised to knock the stuffing out of the ball. The world is full of good bullpen pitchers."

"Would pitching batting practice help you?"

"A little, perhaps, but the attitude of a batter during practice, when he's swinging free and loose, and his attitude during a game when he's tense and alert, are completely different. The situations just aren't comparable."

"Was there any particular kind of pitch that you blame for your sore arm?" asked Nelson.

"I don't believe so, though I know some pitchers will blame their curve or their slider. And the other way, too—when their arm is sore they may claim they can throw the fast ball but not the curve. Not with me, though. When my arm was bad, everything was bad, and when my arm was good, everything was pretty good."

"How's your arm now?" Nelson inquired.

"Just fine." Hart looked at him closely. "Did you have any particular reason for asking?"

"Oh, not really. But I always wondered what I could do against a big league pitcher, and I've never had a chance to find out."

"You can find out today, if you really want to," Hart offered. "That is, if an ex-big league pitcher will qualify."

"He sure would," said Nelson excitedly. "That's the closest I've ever been able to come. Should we go now—"

"Hold the countdown," Ted urged him. "This is an interview and I've not finished yet. Would you go back to the big leagues, Mr. Hart, if you had the opportunity?"

"No, Ted, I don't think so," said the pitcher very quietly. "I think I've had it. If that were my ambition, I would still be active in the minor leagues."

"I've often wondered why pitchers aren't better batters," Nelson remarked. "How do you account for it?"

"I've heard the explanations usually given–that the pitcher has less chance for practice, that he's too busy concentrating on his own job and watching the other pitcher. But I don't think those are the most important reasons. It seems to me that it's a matter of selection. Now you've seen amateur games, particularly the lower classes such as E and F. Who's the best player on the team?"

"The pitcher, usually."

"Yes, and usually it isn't just his pitching that is outstanding. He's generally the best batter, too. Physically, he's usually the strongest, most advanced of the boys, and this helps him become the best all-around athlete. This works out as long as the team is only playing two games a week. But when he breaks into the pro leagues, what happens? Certainly he can't pitch every day. Some players try to pitch every fourth day and play some other position on the other days, but that never lasts very long. The pitcher is the hardest-working player on the team, and after a long game he's used up. It isn't just his arm, either. That means that if he plays another position the next day, he won't be quite up to par. So then, he has to make up his mind. Is he a pitcher or is he something else? If he is of more value as a regular player than he is a pitcher, then that is what he is going to choose. Other things being equal, most players would prefer to play every day. It's more fun, and they feel the opportunities are greater. It's usually only if they feel their batting isn't good enough to earn them a major league berth that they decide to remain pitchers. So once this original choice is made, you can see that pitchers, as a group, are generally inferior batters."

"That makes sense," Nelson agreed.

Much as Ted would have liked to prolong this interview, he finally got to his feet. Nelson also jumped up, remembering Hart's promise.

"Did you mean it–about pitching to me?"

"Sure," Hart assured him.

At the practice field Nelson soon had a bat in his hands. "Would you mind if I let Ted pitch a few to me first? I'd like to get warmed up."

"Surely, and I'd like to warm up myself. We'll make this a really fair test."

Nelson had been an outstanding athlete at Forestdale High School, though more active in football than in baseball. Still, he might have been playing Class A or B amateur baseball himself that summer, had not his college schedule interfered.

There were plenty of other players standing around. One of them acted as a warm-up catcher for Hart, and others were willing to chase any balls which Nelson might hit out of Ted's reach. At first Nelson swung easily, hitting the ball directly back to Ted. But soon he was swinging a little harder, still trying to meet the ball firmly, and Ted was seldom able to field the ball.

"All right, now a few hard ones," Nelson ordered.

"My fast ball or my curve?" asked Ted with a grin.

"What's the difference?" Nelson retorted.

Then Nelson really teed off. He hit several solid line drives, and then one long fly which would normally have gone into deep left field, though it was over the fence running alongside the football field.

"All ready?" asked Hart, as Nelson stepped out of the box a moment to rest. "Then I am, too. I never needed a long time to warm up."

The boy who had been acting as a catcher for Hart now added the full catchers' equipment to his outfit and crouched behind the plate, taking Hart's practice pitches from the mound. As Hart signaled that he had had enough, the catcher called:

"Batter up!"

Nelson stepped back into the box and swung his bat tentatively. Hart wound up. The ball came in, a sizzler. Nelson—

who had at least taken the precaution of putting on a batter's helmet—never even saw it. But he stepped right back into the box for the next pitch, gripping the bat with renewed determination.

Hart wound up again. This time Nelson knew what he was up against, and didn't let the ball out of his sight for as much as a split second. At least he saw it all right, he claimed, but his swing was late and futile.

The ball was returned to the pitcher, and he wound up again. It was another fast ball, and Nelson swung in time. The only trouble was that he missed it by a foot.

"I guess that's strike three," he admitted, dropping his bat.

"No, only strike two," Hart reminded him. "Nobody called the first one."

So Nelson returned to the batter's box. He was more than ever determined to hit that fast ball this time, except that this time it was a curve. And such a wide, sweeping curve Nelson had never seen before. He swung, but came nowhere near it. He didn't even know, as he told Ted later, whether it was over the plate. At first it seemed about to hit him, and then to curve about a foot outside. Even the catcher was fooled, and missed it.

"I don't think I could have hit that if I'd been swinging a barn door," Nelson remarked.

"Oh, come on, the fun's just starting," Hart coaxed him from the mound. "You're not going to leave so soon, are you?"

That had certainly been Nelson's intention, but there was a slightly sarcastic note in Hart's voice that got him. He returned to the batter's box, tapping the edge of the plate.

"Maybe you'll do better if I tell you what's coming," Hart offered. "Don't worry, I won't cross you up. This one is going to be a fast ball."

It was, but Nelson swung with no better luck than before.

"Now a curve," said Hart, and though Nelson knew what to expect, his bat met nothing but empty air.

"So far I haven't been fair—I've been aiming at the corners," Hart told him. "Now I'll tell you right where I'm going to put it. This will be a fast ball, right across the letters."

The ball came and Nelson swung. For the first time he got a piece of the ball, and hit a little foul pop back of the plate. A cheer went up from the spectators.

"Now a curve, breaking right across the center of the plate," said Hart, and delivered to the spot promised. Nelson swung and missed.

"I'll give you another fast one, across the letters again. See if you can do more with it than last time."

But Nelson had begun to do a little thinking for himself. If he couldn't hit this pitcher, if the fast ball was too fast for him to swing and the curve broke too sharply, then he wouldn't try to swing. He'd simply stick out his bat. He did, and met the ball for a perfect little bunt down third, which he would have certainly beaten out unless the third baseman had been playing shallow.

Hart looked surprised, but was willing to continue with the rules he had set up.

"Another fast ball, but low."

Knowing what was coming, Nelson crouched a little lower. Again he managed a neat bunt that would surely have been a successful sacrifice, and might have been a hit.

"Now you're getting on to it," Hart encouraged him. "A low-breaking curve this time."

Nelson stuck out his bat as before, but missed the ball entirely. Half a dozen more pitches were thrown. Nelson found he could generally bunt successfully on a fast ball, but the curve was still an unsolved mystery to him.

"One more—a high fast ball," Hart told him.

Nelson didn't want to bunt again. Since this was the last pitch, why not swing away and see what he could do with it? He did but missed it cleanly. Hart walked off the mound, and came over to him.

"Thanks, Mr. Hart," said Nelson, extending his hand, and the pitcher took it.

"You didn't do so badly, Nelson. You were starting to get on to me toward the end–the way the big leaguers were."

"It took nerve to stand in there against your fast ball," Ted remarked. "Did you ever throw bean balls, Mr. Hart?"

Hart smiled. "Is this for publication?"

"It might be."

"Then, for publication, no, I never did. But off the record, the bean ball wasn't one of my standard pitches. I only used it when I felt obliged to in self-defense. But there are occasions when a pitcher feels it a good thing to let the batters *think* he may throw the bean ball, just the way he likes them to think he uses a spitter."

Hart was soon surrounded with younger boys, and Ted and Nelson left.

"Boy, I feel like a great big dope," Nelson decided. "How many people were watching me?"

"About fifty, at a guess."

"It seemed more like five hundred. If I'd just had more practice this summer, maybe I could have done better. But no, I guess not–not practicing with the kind of players I'd be up against. They only throw about half as fast, and their curves are just optical illusions. It would really take practice to hit Hart's curve. You've got to swing where it isn't, and you don't know if it's going to be a fast ball, in which case you've got to swing before it's there. Say," he added with a sudden thought, "you aren't going to write this up for the paper, are you?"

"Would you mind if I did?"

"Why, sure I'd mind. You think I want the whole town to know how lousy I am?" Then he laughed, as his sense of humor came to his rescue. "Oh, what's the difference? I guess after all it's an honor to strike out against Jack Hart. Who else do we know that's done it?"

"I don't think you were too bad," Ted reassured him. "I've got more confidence in you than you've got in yourself."

☯

8   More Mischief

Anxious though he was to get back to the newspaper office while his interview with Jack Hart was fresh in his mind, Ted had been absent from headquarters for some time, and felt obliged to check in there first. The clerical staff, headed by Margaret Lake, was doing an excellent job, but there were inevitable tangles and some mistakes, most of them not their fault, but which had to be straightened out just the same.

All the teams in the tournament had now reported in, and those that had lost yesterday afternoon and evening, or on this Tuesday morning, were gradually checking out.

At last Ted was able to get over to the *Town Crier* office, and described his interview to Mr. Dobson.

"How much space do you think you can give me?" he concluded, knowing this information would be helpful before he started writing his story.

"Well, Ted, I believe we'll run an extra four pages on Friday and give this tournament the best possible coverage as long as we have so many visitors here. What would you say to twelve inches for your interview?"

"I'd say thanks!" said Ted happily, having expected to get no more than half as much space.

"How's Nelson doing with his camera?"

"Well, he's always got his camera on his mind, but he's been busy with scoring, too. But that will end today. In the semifinal and final rounds they'll be using just the two more experienced scorers, unless a substitute is needed, so he won't have much to do there. But he thought you'd prefer pictures of the later rounds, and he didn't know about those extra four pages. I'll tell him about them right away."

"Do that, Ted. How do you think the Forestdale Rangers are going to make out?"

Ted shook his head doubtfully. "They'll be up against some stiff competition, especially if they should meet the Stanton Bearcats in the final round. Stanton has a pretty solid team, and they play rough, too."

"I've heard that there was some bean-ball throwing last night. Did you see it?"

"I saw something that looked very much like it. Nelson tells me it was worse before I got there, until the Bearcats built up a lead. What do you think about it, Mr. Dobson?"

The editor considered carefully before answering. "I don't want to appear too moralistic about it, Ted, but I don't believe there should be a deliberate effort to injure a player in any sport. It is up to the persons in charge to see that things don't get out of hand," he said firmly and picked up the phone.

Ted was able to spend an uninterrupted hour at his desk, and so had his story in pretty good shape, although it would require a little work later. He mentioned Nelson in a way that he thought would satisfy him; after all, it *was* rather heroic to stand up against a major leaguer's fast ball. And if there was a possibility that Hart was not quite as fast as when he had been in the big leagues, there was also a chance that his control wasn't as good, either.

Then Mr. Dobson had another story to show him written by Carl Allison. There was a good deal of rivalry between Ted and Carl, and to a limited extent the editor encouraged it, thinking that it helped keep both of them on their toes. However, he would never have showed Ted in advance a story written by Carl, unless he had a good reason for wanting Ted's advice. In this instance it was clear why he had consulted Ted, for the story concerned the three cases of juvenile crime which had come up since the tournament teams had begun to arrive in Forestdale. Carl's information had come from the police reports which he checked as part of his regular duties. He had placed the broken jewelry-store window in the lead as being the most important item, followed by the forced entry into the office next door, and concluded with the theft of the model airplane. Even then his story did not close with the familiar "30" to tell the printer this was the end of the story. He left it open in case he had something more to add to it later.

"What do you think of it, Ted?" asked Mr. Dobson. "You were there at the meadow this morning, and you were on the scene shortly after the other two happenings. Is it accurate?"

"Oh, I guess it's accurate enough," Ted decided. "Everything must be the work of juveniles. I saw the boy who stole the plane, and witnesses saw the boys in the other two cases."

"Well, then, what's the matter, Ted?" asked Mr. Dobson.

"It's just that—well—reading the story you get the impression that nothing like this ever happened in Forestdale under normal conditions, and that it's just since the tournament that we've suddenly been struck with a crime wave."

"I know, Ted," said the editor. "It's an example of telling the truth literally, and yet not conveying the truth to the reader."

"Are you going to use the story?" Ted inquired, knowing that Carl would be annoyed enough if anyone changed his story, and ready to blow the roof off if he knew it had been changed because of Ted's advice.

"I can't tell yet. Certainly a great many people know about these happenings already, and if I don't mention them, readers will accuse me of suppressing the news. Well, we'll wait to see what happens by Thursday morning. I'm hoping that if I must use it, at least I'll have several more pleasant stories to go along with it, telling how considerate our visitors have been."

Having finished with his newspaper chores, Ted had his choice of where to go next. The three teams in which he was most interested, the Rangers, the Bearcats, and the Eaglets, were all idle today. He had a hometown loyalty toward the Rangers, had several reasons for hoping the Bearcats would lose, and the conversation of his house guests had won him over to the Eaglets.

A Class A game was available at Eastgate, but Nelson was scoring a Class D game at Westgate, and Ted decided he had better get out there and tell him of the newspaper's need for more pictures.

He was not far from the fire station on his way to Westgate when he heard the fire alarm. He stood close to the driveway, a crowd of excited boys around him, as the firemen ran to their positions and the engine pulled out. One of the boys pointed out a thick column of smoke which seemed to be coming from a line of commercial buildings about five blocks over. Most of the boys took off at a trot in pursuit of the engine, and Ted wondered what he ought to do. There didn't seem to be much of a newspaper story for him, since Carl could easily pick it up later on his regular rounds. On the other hand, Ted recognized the value of a firsthand report, for even Carl's juvenile-crime story indicated to his trained eye that the reporter had not been on the scene at the time of the happenings.

So he turned toward the scene of the fire. Hang it, he thought, maybe it was a sense of duty or a hunch that helped him decide to go, but the main factor was excitement and curiosity. Yet it appeared to be only a small fire, and the chances were that it would be out before he even arrived.

This proved to be very nearly the case, and he found the firemen getting ready to shut off their hoses and wind them up as he approached. The location of the fire was an alleyway running behind a line of commercial buildings. He went around into the alley, the firemen letting him through as a newspaper reporter, though they were stopping other people. The fire seemed to have been confined to a rubbish container in the rear of one of the buildings. Though a small matter, it might have been serious had the fire happened to catch on to the building against which the container stood.

One of the firemen was busy questioning a very excited

man, who gestured wildly as he talked. Ted recognized the man as the proprietor of a small laboratory.

"I saw these boys—wearing baseball uniforms they were—walking through here about half an hour ago. They stopped just outside the back door of my shop. I heard them and looked out, and they saw me and moved on their way."

"What do you think happened?" asked the fireman quietly.

"I think they tossed a match into the container and that it caught on fire. Only it smouldered for a while, so I didn't actually notice the smoke until half an hour later. And it was a good thing I did notice it, too, because the metal container was right up against the wooden wall, and might have set it on fire."

"You didn't actually see them toss a match?"

"No, but I did hear them say something about a strike or striking."

The fireman smiled a little. "Isn't it possible that they were talking about baseball?"

"Well, maybe," the proprietor agreed, having calmed down a little. After all, Ted could hardly blame him. Probably all the capital he possessed was tied up in this small business of his, and if it were burned out he might have faced financial ruin, to say nothing of the possibility that the whole block might have gone up in flames and people been hurt.

"You realize that these rubbish containers shouldn't be right up against a wooden wall," the fireman pointed out, "and there seems to be an unwarranted accumulation of debris here anyway. It represents a fire hazard, and I'm counting on you to clear it up."

"I intended to do it today," the proprietor explained. "But that still isn't doing anything about those boys."

"You say you didn't recognize them?" asked the fireman.

"No, but they were wearing some kind of baseball uniforms, and they were all alike. Doesn't that help any?"

Ted and the fireman looked at each other and tried not to

smile. With probably something like four hundred baseball players in town at that very moment, the chance of locating the offenders on the basis of this slender clue did not look promising.

"Even if we could identify the boys, we don't have any proof that they started the fire," the fireman pointed out.

"Of course they started it. They were hanging around here. Either they did it before I came to the door, or else they came back and did it later because they thought I chased them away." He turned to Ted. "I never liked the idea of Mr. Dobson's inviting all those boys to our town. It was a neat, orderly place until they got here."

Ted did not remind him that the alleyway, at least, was not as neat and orderly as it should have been. The proprietor turned back to the fireman.

"Anyway I know that rubbish doesn't start burning by itself."

"Did you ever hear of spontaneous combustion?"

"I've heard of it," the man agreed, "but I never had any trouble with it. If you can't prove those boys started the fire, can't you at least get them for trespassing?"

"There's no sign up warning them to keep out," the fireman reminded him. "And I suppose this would represent a shortcut for some of the players. Anyway, I have to get the engine back to the station now, but I'll send out an inspector later to talk with you."

Ted and the fireman walked together toward the end of the alleyway.

"You think it was deliberate?" Ted questioned.

"Well, Ted, maybe not so much deliberate as careless or mischievous. I suppose there are plenty of boys who think it smart to toss a lighted match into a rubbish container. It's supposed to contain only noninflammable material, but there might be something there to catch on fire, and if there happened to be something explosive as well, they might get much more excitement than they bargained for. It's true that this is an off day for many of the baseball players, isn't it?"

"Yes, the teams that won yesterday are just marking time."

"Well, boys with nothing much to do, and in a small town that doesn't offer any great possibilities for either exploration or adventure, might find themselves bored, and suddenly there's trouble."

"Mr. Cook certainly was excited, wasn't he?"

"He was, indeed. I wonder if he was afraid *he* might get blamed for the fire, and was anxious to shift the blame. Anyway, the fact that the boys were in uniform suggests that they *do* have a game today, and weren't exactly bored."

Much as he would have liked to clear the boys of blame, Ted was obliged to shake his head. "They may have been heading toward the practice field. It would be a shortcut there, too."

"Yes, that's right," agreed the fireman. "I was thinking if we knew what teams were playing this afternoon that might narrow our search."

"Then you do think it was the fault of the boys and intend to follow it up?"

"I'll wait for the inspector's report, Ted, before I decide what to do. If he finds evidence of a crime, it will be turned over to the police. Right now my responsibility is to keep this engine available every possible minute."

The engine drove off, and Ted went on to Westgate.

"You're late, Ted," Nelson greeted him. "Was there a fire?"

Ted knew he had heard the siren, and quickly explained.

"That's tough," was Nelson's comment, but he obviously had something more immediate on his mind. "You've been missing something, Ted. This pitcher's got a no-hitter going, and he's been striking out batters like crazy."

☯

9   A Long Day

Glancing at the chalkboard hanging on the backstop, Ted observed that this was only the last half of the sixth inning.

"Isn't it early to get excited about a no-hitter?"

"Not the way this pitcher's been going. These batters haven't been able to buy a base hit. They've been swinging their bats as though they were waving good-bye to their mothers."

Ted began watching the game with growing interest. The pitcher did look pretty good to him.

"He is fast, isn't he?" Ted decided.

"Well, nothing *really* looks fast to me any more after batting against Hart, but I'd say he's very fast for his class, and tricky besides. What did I tell you?" he added, as the batter went down swinging, retiring the side.

The boy with the chalk wrote in a zero for the last half of the sixth inning. The Bohunks held only a one-run lead, however, in spite of their pitcher's excellent performance.

"I wonder where they got that name?" Ted speculated. "It isn't exactly dignified."

"I was talking to some of the players before the game. Someone hung it on them as a kind of sarcastic nickname, but they decided they liked it, and adopted it."

The Bohunks added a run in their half of the seventh, giving their pitcher a slightly more comfortable margin to work with. Then he took the mound again, apparently as fresh and determined as ever, to judge by the way he zipped in his warm-up pitches. He wasn't relaxing even then.

The first batter seemed to have decided to wait the pitcher

out, hoping either for a base on balls or that he might be given a "cripple" if the pitcher got behind on him. But the pitcher did not get behind. The first pitch was a called strike, the second a ball. The batter shortened up as though to bunt the next pitch, but held back, though the umpire called it a strike anyway. Then another fast ball came in, the batter seemed to hesitate as though undecided, but was called out on strikes.

"What did you think of that bunt try, Ted?" asked Nelson, as he wrote down something in his scoring book.

"He didn't really bunt," Ted reminded him.

"No, but he had half a notion to. I think we may see a change of tactics. They can't hit this pitcher with a full swing, so they'll try to bunt him. I know that's what I'd tell them to do, if I were the manager."

Nelson was right for the next batter obviously was there for the purpose of bunting and nothing more. He bunted at the first pitch and missed. The second one went foul back. There was momentary doubt if he would attempt to bunt on the third strike, but he soon made it pretty obvious by the way he had shortened up on his bat. He did bunt and met the ball well, but it rolled foul down the third-base line. He was out and the pitcher was credited with a strikeout.

The following batter also tried to bunt, with the difference that he took a full swing after he had two strikes. He met the ball partially this time, and popped out to the infield.

The Bohunks failed to score in the top of the eighth, and their pitcher took the mound once more.

"I wonder if he realizes he's working on a no-hitter?" Ted mused.

"Of course he does. There hasn't even been anything that looked like a hit so far."

"What about this tradition that a pitcher is never reminded he hasn't allowed any hits so far?"

"I think that's baloney, Ted. Maybe his own team does it, though I should think that would make him all the more tense when his team mates stop talking to him. But what about the other team? Don't you suppose they're constantly calling out to the pitcher about it, trying to upset him? What are they supposed to do, agree to let him have his no-hitter and pretend they don't care whether they win or lose?"

"I don't hear much of that coming from the other bench," Ted observed.

"No, in these amateur games the managers try to keep the bench jockeying down a little. They think it keeps their own players from concentrating on the game the way they should. Oh–oh."

"What's the matter?"

"That third baseman. What's he playing so deep for? He knows they'll try to bunt again."

"He can't be sure, Nel. Maybe if he comes in too close they'll slam it right through him and part his hair."

"Well, he oughtn't to be back that far," Nelson muttered. "A well-placed bunt and he'd be out of luck."

As Nelson had foretold, the first batter bunted away, meeting the ball well but a little too hard. It rolled close to the right of the third-base bag. The third baseman picked it up and hurled it to first with a single motion for the put-out.

"A good fielding play," Ted remarked.

"Sure it was. He's a good fielder. But he's just asking for trouble if he plays that far back again. This next batter is going to bunt, sure as shootin'."

And the batter did. After letting a ball go by, and missing one, he stuck his bat out so that it barely met the ball, which went directly along the third-base foul line, finally rolled fair, and settled about halfway between home plate and the third-base bag. The pitcher had no chance for it, nor did the catcher, and at a call from one of the players they stopped dead in their tracks. It was up to the third baseman to get it, and the best thing they could do was to stay out of his way.

The third baseman raced in, picked up the ball, pivoted . . . and held on to the ball. Just why he did not attempt the throw in any case no one knew. Maybe he thought it was foul, maybe he decided it was too late, or maybe he found he did not have a good grip on the ball. A mixed chorus of cheers and groans went up from the crowd.

"How about it?" Ted demanded.

"A base hit," said Nelson quietly, and made the necessary notations on his scoring sheet. "I think the runner would have had it beaten out, even if he made the throw."

"But he was out of position," Ted argued. "You pointed that out yourself."

"I can't help that. Being caught out of position isn't the same thing as an error—unless it involves the failure to cover a base. Every hit in a ball game—unless the ball's high up against the fence or over it—means that somebody was out of position. That is, the ball *could* have been caught, if a fielder had happened to be stationed right there. The catch is that the fielders can't be everywhere, and the batter shows his skill when he manages to hit the ball to a spot where he has noticed an opening in the defense."

"Somebody's going to hate you," Ted reminded him.

"This is going to be one of those days when I hate myself. Let's hope that these boys come up with just one good, clean hit and take me off the spot."

But he was not to have his wish in that inning. The next two batters both bunted. But the third baseman, who had overestimated his ability to get in on a bunt, had now learned his lesson, played in closer, and fielded them smoothly.

As the inning ended, the manager of the Bohunks left the bench and came over to the stands to talk to Nelson.

"How did you score that play, Morgan?" he inquired.

"A base hit," said Nelson firmly, though with some reluctance.

"Well, that's the way it looked to me, too, but I was hoping that maybe I was wrong."

"Maybe we're both wrong," Nelson returned, "but that's how I saw it."

At this point, Ted had a chance to tell Nelson about Mr. Dobson's plans for the special four-page baseball spread in the paper, and Nelson brightened up.

"That's great. I wasn't planning on really getting started with pictures until tonight, but maybe I'd better do it right now. Would you get my camera from the car for me, Ted? I can't afford to miss any of the game. If I can get a picture of this pitcher in the paper, maybe it will make it up to him for the no-hitter he missed."

Ted was back with the camera in a few minutes. Very little had happened, and the Bohunks went down one-two-three.

In the last of the ninth, the Bohunk pitcher seemed to have lost a little of his stuff. He undoubtedly knew of the scorer's decision against him, and either it discouraged him or else he was just growing tired. The batters stopped bunting, and began to swing away, meeting the ball well, but in each case it went directly to a fielder. The game ended with a long fly ball to the center fielder.

"Just that one lousy little hit," said Nelson bitterly. "I wonder if that pitcher feels any worse about it than I do."

"You had to call it the way you saw it," Ted reminded him.

"Sure I did. But I'd much rather be honest where it does somebody some good. What good did it do to take that pitcher's no-hitter away from him?"

"What about the other team? You had to be fair to them."

"What difference does it make? If you lose with just a few hits, people think how bad your team was. But when you lose on a no-hitter, they forget about that and think how good the other team was. Of course that batter was entitled to his hit."

But then Ted saw something, and gave Nelson a sharp nudge. It wasn't the pitcher who felt bad. He was out there giving the third baseman a pat on the back. Nelson immediately felt better, and probably so did everyone else in the park who noticed it.

Nelson took a few pictures, while most of the Bohunks

stood around and watched. After all, they *did* win the game, and that was the important thing, though they had momentarily forgotten it in their disappointment over the no-hitter.

"Well, just one more game for me to score," said Nelson as he packed up his equipment. "I'll summarize this, and then turn it in to the office. This is sure one job I'll be glad to get rid of. Then I can concentrate on taking pictures. What do you have to do, Ted?"

"Check in at the office, first thing. Then I thought maybe I'd stop in at the fire house and see if there's any further information about that rubbish fire. Then home for supper."

"And tonight? There's a big Class A game over at Eastgate. Going to take it in?"

"I'd like to, but aren't you scoring the Class D game here? I want to look in on that a little, anyway. Maybe the game will end early and we can both go over to Eastgate."

"That game may run under the lights. Do you care?"

"No—what difference does it make as long as the lights work? That will extend the playing time at least an hour, and they can go on and play even after it's completely dark if they want to. The lights may not be up to big league standards, but they're not so bad, either. In fact the infield is pretty good."

"Remember when we were kids how we used to play baseball by the light of a street lamp? I wonder why we never got our heads taken off?"

"Maybe because the batters couldn't see the ball any better than the fielders."

There was not a great deal to do at the office. Nelson worked on his scorebook while Ted took care of other duties. In half an hour they were ready to leave. At the fire house they found the same fireman on duty whom Ted had talked to earlier.

"Yes, the inspector did go out there," he replied in answer to Ted's question, "and I think we've got the whole thing cleared up now. After Mr. Cook finally calmed down, the inspector was able to get a straight story out of him, look over the evidence, and consult the partner. You know they have some small industrial furnaces there which they use for some of their chemical processes. Well, the partner worked on something during the night, then took out the ashes and put them in the rubbish container. Later Mr. Cook threw out some plastic containers, not realizing the ashes were still hot. They smouldered for hours, before finally breaking into flame. You remember that peculiar odor there, don't you, Ted? I should have recognized it as plastic. Anyway, the boys had nothing whatever to do with it."

After thanking the fireman, they left the station–Ted, at least, feeling much relieved.

"It just goes to prove that these visiting boys aren't responsible for *everything* that goes wrong while they're here."

"No," Nelson agreed, "but remember, Ted, that just because they were innocent here doesn't clear them of everything. Somebody *did* enter the office, the jewelry-store window *was* broken, and that model airplane is still missing."

"I know. I'm just glad that Carl won't have more ammunition to put into his story."

He went on to tell Nelson about the story Carl had written. Ted often spoke of Carl as being deliberate and cautious, but Nelson called him "pigheaded."

"So that's what he's up to," was Nelson's reaction. "How does Mr. Dobson go for it?"

"I'd say he doesn't exactly like it, but as long as Carl is telling the truth, he doesn't want to suppress it, either. A story like that is certainly important enough to appear in a small-town paper like ours."

"Anything we can do about it, Ted? If we could find out who did some of those things, it might help."

"It might. At least we'd know whom to blame, instead of blaming everybody in general. But how are we going to find out? In every case the boys were seen, but not well enough to be identified. About the only hope I can see would be to catch the boy with the airplane red-handed. But we can't even do that with the others, because they didn't get away with anything that we know of."

"What about the curfew, Ted? The boys who entered the office were out after hours. Couldn't we check up and see?"

Ted considered, but shook his head doubtfully. "It would be a big job to begin with, and I don't really think it would lead to anything. I imagine they got out of the house, or the hotel, or wherever they were staying, without anyone realizing they were gone. And even if we came up with a case where the boys *might* have been out, we'd still have trouble proving they were the ones who broke into the office."

"Got any ideas?" asked Nelson, after a short pause.

"Nothing very good, I guess. I just wish we had some idea of why those boys broke into headquarters. If we had the answer to that question, we might be able to identify them with very little trouble."

Cal and Larry were at home for supper when Ted arrived. They planned to see the Class A game at Eastgate that evening, the game to be followed by a fireworks exhibition. They were anxious to give Ted any help he needed, but he assured them that Cliff would have no cots to move that night and could handle things for himself. Ted promised that he himself would probably be at Eastgate before the game was over, and this satisfied them.

Some duties at the office detained Ted, and he arrived at Westgate when the game was already more than half over, taking his seat beside Nelson. The stands were not crowded, since the game at Westgate was not the big attraction.

"Any trouble?" he inquired.

"Nothing at all," Nelson returned. "But it's been an interesting game, and I think I'd get good and excited about it if I knew the players a little better."

"Then they wouldn't have had you score the game," Ted reminded him.

"Well, I'll be glad when it's over. That business this afternoon bothered me, and I'll be much better satisfied when I can get to work on my camera."

"We've been awfully lucky, haven't we? There hasn't been a suggestion of rain, and all the games have moved ahead smoothly and on schedule. I don't believe there has been more than one extra-inning game, and that was only one inning."

"It's been a pretty nip-and-tuck thing, Ted. One thing that speeded things up was that very few of these amateur players like to wait for a base on balls. Maybe they think it's kind of cowardly, or maybe they are so afraid of striking out that they figure they need their three swings."

"Or maybe they just like to hit that ball," said Ted with a grin.

"Anyway, anything Mr. Dobson runs usually does turn out all right. He's lucky, but by being efficient he helps to make his own luck. And I'll bet that even if we'd had a cloudburst, he'd have worked things out somehow."

It was nearly twilight as the game ended. Nelson gladly put his scorebook away, and took a few pictures of the players with his flash. Then they left in his car for Eastgate. They found that the game there had been interrupted in order to turn on the lights. Ted held his breath for a moment, but was relieved to see the lights come on. In a few minutes the umpires ordered resumption of play.

It was an overflow crowd, and more spectators were still arriving in anticipation of the fireworks. Ted found standing room only, but Nelson went down on the field with his camera, getting as close to the field of action as the umpires would allow him in quest of action shots.

"What I wouldn't give for a sequence camera," he remarked to Ted during a brief interval when they got together. "This way the picture you get is often just a little too early or a little too late."

But he was happy anyway, and made at least a dozen shots.

Then the game ended, the lights were turned off, and the fireworks began. Twenty minutes later they, too, were over, and the crowd began to disperse. Nelson offered Larry and Cal a lift home, but they were with some of their friends and said they preferred to walk. Ted made a final check at headquarters, and locked up for the night.

"Where to now, Ted?" asked Nelson. "Are you tired?"

"Tired, but not sleepy. I'd like to unwind a little. This day's been about a week long."

"Then what do you say we take a little ride out in the country to cool off?"

"OK, let's go."

It was nearly midnight when they returned from their ride. Most of the houses in town were dark, or had a single light still on. But they were surprised to notice one house that seemed to have every light in it burning.

"Isn't that Fred Ewer's house?" asked Nelson. "Want to go and see?"

"I sure do," Ted replied.

They drove slowly by the Ewer home. There was a strange car in the drive, an expensive model they knew did not belong to the Ewer family, but that was the only clue as to what was happening.

"What do you think, Ted?"

"I think that I'm going to check there the first thing in the morning. Now let's get home and go to bed. It's going to be a big day tomorrow."

10 Ted's Scoop

At nine o'clock sharp Ted and Nelson drove up in front of the Ewer home.

"Think we're too early?" Ted wondered. "I'd hate to get them out of bed."

"The way they were going last night, I doubt if they even went to bed. You think this really is what we think it is, Ted?"

"Sure looks like it."

"But what are you going to do if we're wrong?"

"Do some fast back-pedaling, I guess. We don't want to tip them off about the scouts if none of them has showed up yet. We'll just ask them about Fred's plans for next summer, or something like that."

Ted rang the bell. It was answered by Mr. Ewer.

"Why, Ted . . ." He hesitated. "I don't know . . ."

But his wife appeared behind him. "Oh, Ted–and Nelson. Come on in, boys. We're glad to have you. I suppose you realize what's happened, and that's why you're here. We promised not to say anything, but if you guessed, I don't see how we could help that."

They were shown into the living room, and Fred soon came downstairs to join them. It didn't take more than a glance to show that he was bubbling over about something.

"We noticed your lights on late last night," Ted began as they were seated, "and we thought–well, you know how rumors get around."

"And this one was right," Fred exploded joyfully. "Can I tell them, Dad?"

"I guess it's all right. It'll have to be."

"Well, then, I'm all signed up for the big leagues! I mean, I've signed up for one of the farm teams, but it ought to lead there in a few years."

Ted and Nelson offered quick congratulations. Then Ted asked:

"What was the name of the scout who signed you?"

"Mr. Hill. Why, do you know him?"

Ted nodded. "We've met him. As a matter of fact, he asked us a few questions about you."

"Then you must have given him the right answers, because he showed up last night with a contract in his pocket. Maybe I've got you to thank for this."

"Nelson had more to do with it than I did," Ted informed him. "He's seen you play more than I have."

"Well, then, thanks, Nel," said Fred, turning to Nelson.

"Oh, I didn't do anything," Nelson protested. "If you made it, you made it on your own ability." He looked a little worried. "But wasn't this rather sudden? I should think you would have waited to see if any other offers came in."

"That might have been wiser," Mr. Ewer spoke up, "but he said he had to leave today. He offered to leave the contract, but he said if we didn't sign, he would have to consider it as unfinished business, and recognize the possibility that some other scout might step in, so he would act accordingly. I called up a lawyer about it, and he said it was all right, so we signed. Mr. Hill told us frankly that if we thought Fred might qualify for a big bonus, then we'd be better off waiting, and that he wouldn't enter into that kind of bid. But unless someone wanted to make Fred a bonus baby, then nobody would offer us anything more than he did. Fred liked this team and this system, so that ended it."

"I didn't want to become a bonus baby," said Fred eagerly. "I mean, I wouldn't turn down a *big* bonus, but I wouldn't want just a little extra bonus that would put me over the limit. Then there're all sorts of restrictions on you, and it interferes with your development. This way I've got a chance to make it on my own."

"What we liked best about it," Mrs. Ewer offered, "is that this offers Fred a chance to go to college. It's entered in his contract that he can leave the team a little early in September, and report a little late in March, if he has to, in order to make his college term. This will give him a complete semester each year, and he can get in a partial semester during the rest of the year studying by extension, so he can complete his college work in six years. That's how long it would take him anyway, if he had to stop to earn some money."

It seemed like a happy arrangement all around, and Ted could find nothing wrong with it. They talked about baseball in general, and about Fred's plans for the future.

"Do you think you'll go on being a switch hitter," Nelson inquired, "or will you finally decide one way or the other?"

"I don't know yet. It will depend on what my coaches advise. I'm a steadier batter right-handed, but have more power left-handed. I can't tell which way to decide it. But when I'm up against better pitching, I may find I do better one way than the other."

"How about letting us have a picture?" Ted suggested.

"I've got my graduation picture, if you want that," Fred mentioned.

"No, I imagine Mr. Dobson would prefer an action shot. Could you put on your uniform and come over to the practice field with us?"

"I sure could. It may be the last time I'll ever put that uniform on. Is it all right if my brother comes along? Maybe he could get in the picture, too."

Hank was still asleep, but Fred awakened him. They both came downstairs in uniform, and drove off with Ted and Nelson. At the field, Nelson posed a number of pictures which might look as though they were taken in action. When Fred was swinging his bat, Hank acted as catcher. He also appeared in a number of other shots.

"But don't expect Mr. Dobson to use more than one of these pictures," said Nelson with a laugh. "There are other baseball players in town, too, you know."

There was no comment from Ted, and Nelson looked up to see that his attention was on a passing car. The driver stuck out his arm and waved at them.

"Ken Kutler," Ted explained, rather annoyed. "Wouldn't you know it? He's just about the one person I didn't want to see us."

"You think he knows what's going on?"

"Sure, he does. Nobody ever has to draw him a map."

Nelson offered to drive Fred and his brother home, but they declined, saying they wanted to watch one of the games. Then Nelson drove Ted slowly back to the office, and they sat in the car for a few minutes before Ted got out.

"It's funny about Fred," Nelson mused. "Sure, he's a good player, but he's not *so* much better than some of the others. Somebody could give you a pretty good argument that he's not even the best player on the team."

"But Mr. Hill must have thought he was a shade better, and it was just that shade he wanted."

"That—and the ability to grow. Everybody knows Fred isn't ready to step into a major league game right now. But Mr. Hill somehow had confidence that he could grow into it. You were counting on this story for a kind of scoop, weren't you, Ted?"

"Yes, I guess I was. It doesn't happen every year that a Forestdale boy gets signed up with a professional contract, and this occurred at just the right time to make a big spread in our baseball section."

"What do you suppose Ken will do about it? After all, it doesn't exactly spoil your story if he gets it, too."

"No, but it'll take off a little of the edge. But that's not what's bothering me. I'm trying to figure Ken out."

"What do you mean?"

Ted began argumentatively, "Why didn't he stop today when he saw us taking Fred's picture?"

"Maybe he was in a hurry."

"He didn't look like he was in very much of a hurry. Anyway, he usually has time to stop for a few words whenever he happens to see me."

"Then he figured you were working on a story and didn't want to interrupt," Nelson suggested.

"Yes, he must have figured I was working on a story, and I don't see how there could be any doubt about what the story was. Even if he didn't recognize Fred, the uniform would have been a giveaway. But you see, he couldn't have figured he was interrupting, because we had both discussed Fred at the scout meeting. It would have been natural for him to join in, but he didn't. So what is he going to do next?"

"He'll probably stop off at Fred's home sometime later and talk with him."

Ted shook his head. "No, I don't think so. Ken would do anything he could to beat me out on a story. But if he knew I had a story, and wanted to find out what it was, and expected to use the same story himself—no, Ken just doesn't work that way. If he knew something I didn't know, that would be his secret. But if I knew something that he didn't, then he wouldn't have a secret. He'd play it out in the open."

"What chapter in our logic book did you get this out of? I must have been asleep that day." Nelson screwed up his face the way he always did when Ted got a little too involved for him. "Then what do you think he is going to do?"

"That's just it, Nel. I don't think he's going to do anything. I think he's just plain *giving* this story to me."

"That doesn't sound like a competitor."

"It wouldn't in a big city, Nel, but this is a little different out here. This is a big story in Forestdale. In North Ridge it would only rate a line or two. So then, why should Ken spoil it for me? He's letting me have it, figuring that the people who are really interested in the story, the people in Forestdale, will get it from the *Town Crier*."

"Well, if Ken's giving you the story, and you think it's all right for him to do it, I can't see what your problem is—unless it's to say thanks!"

Ted remained thoughtful. "But that brings up another problem. I wondered why Ken took me to that scouts' meeting, but after I learned they were interested in Fred Ewer, I thought that explained it. Maybe it did, for me. But if Ken wasn't interested in Fred Ewer, then why was *he* at the meeting?"

"Curiosity, maybe."

"It could be, but I've learned through hard experience that Ken usually has some purpose in mind when he does something. And then I keep harping back to that conversation I had with him last Sunday. He hinted that gamblers might be interested in these games, and warned me that everyone who pretended to be a scout might not really be one."

"Ken really is a friend, isn't he?"

"I don't think he would have told me that just because I was a newspaper reporter. He did it, I believe, because of my part in this baseball tournament and his hope that nothing would go wrong. That *was* friendship—no doubt about that."

Nelson was beginning to get a glimmer. "If he told you a scout might be a fake, do you think he had Mr. Hill in mind? Then maybe Fred's signed to a fraudulent contract, or one that perhaps has been misrepresented in some way. That could be real trouble for him, couldn't it?"

"It could. But remember his father said they consulted a lawyer before signing it. And besides, I think if it was something like that, Ken would have stopped off today and tried to get to the bottom of it. It seems more likely to me that it's one of the other two men, Mr. Saunders or Mr. Scotch."

"But which one, Ted?"

Ted laughed. "Yes, that's the problem. Which one? Or

maybe it's neither of them and I'm all wet. What did you think of Mr. Saunders and Mr. Scotch?"

"They seemed all right to me. They were sort of quiet and intelligent. If you'd asked me that before, I would have said that Mr. Hill was the blowoff and the one to watch carefully. Still, he was the one who signed Fred up, so he must be a scout if the contract is all right. Can't you wait and see whether Mr. Saunders or Mr. Scotch approach Fred with a proposition?"

"I imagine it's too late for that. Word gets around in these things, and if they are legitimate scouts, they probably know that Fred is already signed up and won't do anything about it. They knew from that meeting yesterday that they would have to act fast. But neither of them did. Maybe they decided against Fred, or maybe they couldn't get the approval of their home offices."

"Or maybe one or both of them is a fake," Nelson concluded. "But just supposing one of them *isn't* a scout, and *is* a gambler, Ted. Then what do we do?"

"I don't know whether there is anything we could do," said Ted thoughtfully. "I hate the idea of gambling, but unless they break the law in some way, and we can prove it, we're out of luck."

"Betting on a sports event is illegal, isn't it?"

"Technically, it is. As Ken said, nobody's going to object to small, friendly wagers. But when professional gamblers move in and set up shop, possibly influencing players, paying off umpires and public officials, and using some of their own unique methods of collecting bad debts, then it's time to do something about it."

"You mean you think all this activity is going on here, in Forestdale, right under Sergeant Jeffers' nose?" asked Nelson incredulously.

"No, all the activity wouldn't be here. But the games are here, and there's a lot of public interest in them all over the state. That means that betting is probably going on. Let's hope that most of it is private and not professional. But where there's enough interest for private betting, the professional gamblers are likely to try to step in, too."

"Then what do you suppose the gamblers would be doing here in Forestdale?"

"That's hard to tell. If either Mr. Saunders or Mr. Scotch is a professional gambler, it might be that he is watching over the operation, collecting data, and passing this information down the line, all over the state. How many ways do you know of to bet on a baseball game, Nel?"

"Well, there's winning-run gambling. You find out in what half-inning the winning run is scored, and whoever had selected that half-inning wins the pool. That's used most in office and factory pools. It's really a kind of lottery, and one thing that's wrong with it is that the winning run is more likely to be scored in a late inning than in an early inning. I don't think professional gamblers would be much interested in that kind of thing.

"There's numbers gambling, too. They might take the winning score in three different baseball games, such as seven-three-six, and then pay off on that number. You'd have one chance in a thousand of winning, and they make their profit by paying off at only four hundred or six hundred to one.

"Then there's the setting up of odds. They might quote three to two on Forestdale, and then accept bets on either side. Or if they figure it's a toss-up, they might quote six to five, and take your choice of either team. If they got exactly equal bets for each team, then they would make a little profit, anyway. Under a good odds system, there will be about equal betting on each side. But gamblers would usually prefer to have the favorite win, because the payoff is less, and because there is less public stir than there is when a favorite is defeated.

"And then there's point-spread betting, though that's more common in football and basketball. They might decide that one team is three runs better than another team. If the favorite team wins by more than three runs, they pay off on it. But if the favorite wins by less than three runs, or maybe loses the game, then they pay off the other side."

"But if they were setting up odds or quoting point spreads," Ted asked, "then that's information that would have to be passed along, isn't it?"

"I guess it is," Nelson decided. "I suppose it couldn't be done too far ahead. After a team has won a big victory or suffered a bad defeat, the odds would immediately change with respect to the next game. They have to be based on all the latest information available."

"Well, I guess that's it," Ted decided, finally getting out of the car. "I suppose we can't stop people from gambling. That's up to the police, anyway. But we can keep our eyes open to make sure they don't interfere with the players. That would be about the worst thing that could happen!"

11 A Confession

Ted found that work was piling up at headquarters. Half the boys in the tournament had already left town, or would be leaving sometime that day. Checking out sometimes involved complications and he was caught up in this activity.

He did find time to slip over to the *Town Crier* office, where he told Mr. Dobson the good news about Fred Ewer. The editor promised to feature the story prominently in their special baseball section, and to use a picture, too, if Nelson could come up with a good one. He also agreed with Ted that Ken had probably deliberately turned the story over to him and was off on the trail of something else.

"And Ted," the editor concluded, "what do you think of sending a copy of Friday's *Town Crier* to each player in the tournament? They could be sent in a bundle to each team's headquarters and distributed from there."

"That's a great idea, Mr. Dobson," said Ted enthusiastically. "I was thinking that some of these players might get their pictures in the paper and never know it, because their teams would have left town by Friday."

"All right, Ted, I'll leave it up to you to get the names and addresses of all the managers and the number of copies required, and put your order in with the printer. Now, what are your plans for today?"

"I guess it's more a question of leaving out the things I won't be able to do. I'd like to get over to the Bearcats' game this morning if I could. Nelson's over there with his camera because he says he hopes to get a picture of them losing. Mr. Wyatt isn't the most agreeable man you'd care to meet, and some of the players seem to be taking their cue from him. Then my two visitors, Larry and Cal, are going to be disappointed if I don't get to their game at one-thirty, and of course everybody wants to see the Rangers' game at four if they can make it."

"Well, do whatever you can, Ted. We must get more copy to the printer today, too, if we're going to get that special section out. We can't wait till the last minute with everything. I'm afraid Carl has a full schedule, but Miss Monroe and I will be ready to help with everything we can. I'd cover the Rangers' game today for you, except that I don't like to take your best story away from you."

"Oh, you'd better take it, Mr. Dobson. I'm going to need help, I can see that. But a lot of the writing is going to depend on what pictures we decide to use. Nelson doesn't have too many yet, but he has some, and he'll have more very soon. I know he put some of them in the developer last night, and he might have a chance to make some prints between games today. It's too bad we won't be able to get the finals in our baseball section, but we'll have all the first-round games, and eight out of the twelve semifinal games."

Ted returned to the baseball office to find the girls beginning to close up the records of the teams that had been eliminated from the tournament. Though they were good at operating the calculating machines, they were confused about the statistics. Ted showed them how to figure baseball averages, and accumulate the other data required. Having got them started, he was about to leave the office when three boys entered. They were not in uniform, but it was apparent that they were among the visiting baseball players, and from their size they were probably in Class F.

Two of the boys hung back a little, while urging the other one forward. He looked around, and decided that Ted was the person he wanted to see.

"Are you the man in charge of the tournament?"

"I'm in charge of the office here," said Ted with a smile. "What can I do for you?"

"Well–" The boy looked at his friends for encouragement or help. He did not get the help he sought, but he did get a couple of nudges that told him to go on. "We wanted to confess!"

"Confess? What did you want to confess?"

"Well, you know that jewelry-store window?"

Ted was startled. "Sure." He pulled out some chairs. "Here, you'd better sit down and we'll talk this over."

The boys sat down on the edges of their seats. The leader, now that he had taken the big step, seemed to have run out of words, and the others certainly weren't going to say anything if they could help it.

"What team are you boys from?" asked Ted.

"The Young'uns."

Ted remembered having run across this team among the eight in Class F. They had won their game on Monday, and were scheduled again for this afternoon.

"All right, we'll talk about the jewelry-store window. What's your name?"

"Dick Hale."

He turned to the other boys, who gave their names as Jackie Centers and Hanley Phillips. Then he turned back to Dick.

"Now, what happened, Dick?"

"Well . . ." Dick took a deep breath and decided he might as well get this over with as fast as he could. "We were standing by this jewelry store, you see. We'd won our game, and Jackie, here, said if we got to be professional baseball players we would be able to buy some of this expensive jewelry for our mothers. And Hanley said his mother's birthday was coming soon, and wouldn't it be nice if he could buy that pretty necklace for her. We looked at the price and it said one-one-oh-oh, but we didn't know whether that meant eleven dollars or one thousand one hundred dollars, and we argued about it, but Hanley said it didn't make any difference because he didn't have eleven dollars, either. So we turned around and were standing there talking about something else, and we must have been sort of sitting on that little ledge in front of the window, when all at once the glass started to crack, and Jackie said, 'Holy cow! Let's get out of here,' and so we ran away, and after that we heard the alarm go off. I guess that's all that happened."

Ted had little doubt that he was hearing an exact account of the accident. These boys might have been able to make up a story, but he did not think they could have made up a convincing conversation to go with it. Besides, there would be no point in making a partial confession. If they wanted to hide the facts of the case, they would have stayed away. But just to be certain, Ted questioned the other boys as well. The facts were substantially the same, but their stories were sufficiently different so that it was obvious they had not rehearsed them in advance.

"What made you decide to confess?" he asked Dick.

"Well, we knew we'd have to pay for the window, but we talked it over, and thought that if we confessed maybe we wouldn't be allowed to play in our game today, and the one on Friday if we win. So we tried to figure out if we could pay for it, and we thought it might cost a hundred dollars. Well, that would be thirty-three dollars and thirty-three cents for each of us and a penny more. We thought maybe we could pay a dollar a month out of our allowances and maybe some more if we could get some jobs to do, and we could have it paid off before three years was up. Do you think they would let us pay for it in installments?"

Ted tried to conceal a smile. "I think very likely they would—if they decide you ought to pay for the window."

"And let us play in our baseball games?"

"I should think so."

Ted stood up suddenly. "All right, boys, come on. We'll take a little walk over to the police station and explain the accident to Sergeant Jeffers."

"Will he arrest us?" asked Hanley with a quaver.

"I don't think so. But he has a report on the broken window, and I'm sure he'd like to close up the case."

Ted stopped to look in at the newspaper office and was pleased to find Carl at his desk.

"Carl," he called, "these three boys are the ones who broke the jewelry-store window, and we're on our way over to the police station to make a report. Want to come along?"

As a matter of principle, Carl usually opposed anything Ted had to suggest, and seemed about to do the same this time. But he hesitated, and then appeared to change his mind.

"All right, I'll come," he said finally.

He and Ted walked along together, leading the way for the three boys, but not saying a word to each other. At the station Ted quickly explained matters to the sergeant. He took out a form and began to write on it as he questioned them.

"That will do, boys," he concluded. "Sit down and wait a few minutes."

The boys did so, though gingerly, and the sergeant walked off a short distance with Ted and Carl.

"I'd say their story sounds pretty good. There's just one detail that doesn't check out. I don't see why a heavy plate-glass window should break just from leaning against it. I'm going to get Mr. Williams over here."

The proprietor arrived within a few minutes. Sergeant Jeffers indicated the three boys who had admitted causing the breaking of the window, but talked with the man outside their hearing.

"They say they broke the window from leaning against it. How does that sound to you?"

Mr. Williams looked cautious. "Well, maybe it *could* have happened that way. I saw them hanging around and thought they broke it with a rock."

"You think now that the window could have been broken by leaning against it, but you didn't say anything like that before. What makes you think so now?"

"Well–" Mr. Williams seemed uneasy. "Maybe I should have told you about it before, but there was a crack in the window. Not a very big crack. It came from the frost last winter, but it didn't seem important enough to put in a claim. I was going to tell the insurance agent the next time he came around to collect the annual premium."

"You're darned right you should have told me about it," said Sergeant Jeffers angrily. "The difference between breaking a jewelry-store window accidentally and breaking it intentionally makes all the difference in the world, as far as the police are concerned."

"Well, then, why did they run away like they did? How could I help but think they were guilty?" asked Mr. Williams.

Nelson had once referred to Carl as pigheaded. But once he was fully convinced he was wrong, he never hesitated to acknowledge his mistake.

"Maybe they've had experience trying to explain things to angry adults, and that's made them careful," he now said. "Incidentally, have you thought that if these boys can prove they were cut by the glass, they might have a claim against you?" Carl turned from Mr. Williams to Ted. "I see where I'm going to have to rewrite a story I was just about ready to turn in to the printer."

He nodded in a friendly way to Ted and the sergeant, and strode out of the station.

"Is that right, what he said about having a claim against me?" asked the jeweler anxiously.

"Well, it's possible. So far they haven't said anything about getting cut, and I don't want to put any ideas into their heads. But it might help if you were to withdraw your complaint."

"Yes, yes, I withdraw it. But I still think you should give them a good scolding. They had no business hanging around my store window. If they were customers it would be different, but they won't be customers for a good many years yet."

Then he, too, left the station. Ted and the officer walked over to where the boys were sitting.

"All right, boys, it's all taken care of," the sergeant informed them. "I'm sure your story of how the window was broken is true. But remember, this whole trouble came about because you ran away. That meant there had to be a police report, and questioning of witnesses, and the police had to be alerted to try to discover which boys did it. You caused us a great deal of trouble and worry just by running away. You won't do it again, will you?"

"No," they answered in a chorus.

"Then you may go."

"Don't you need our names?" asked Dick.

"That won't be necessary. Mr. Williams has canceled his complaint."

"Won't we have police records?" Hanley inquired worriedly.

"No," said Ted.

"But don't we have to pay for the window?" Jackie wanted to know.

"No, the window was insured. Now run along and try to win your game this afternoon."

The boys were glad to go, and Ted followed their example.

He was late for the Bearcats' game, and was rather surprised to find Nelson sitting in the first row of the stands instead of crouching with his camera out on the field.

"What's the matter?" asked Ted, sitting down beside him.

"Oh, who wants pictures of this game? Notice the score?"

Ted looked, and saw that the Bearcats were leading, seven to one. The game was in the seventh inning, so that it looked as though the Bearcats were due for another victory, unless the Bobtails could suddenly rise up and do something.

"Then why are you here? Mr. Dobson's going to need pictures, and need them fast. You could be out at Westgate."

"I know. I took a few pictures, and I'll be able to make some contact prints during lunchtime. But I just feel like hanging around here to see what's going to happen. They're at it again."

"What, bean balls?"

"You called the ticket, mister. Every time they're in a little bit of a jam, that old bean ball comes out. You'd think with a lead like that, they'd lay off, but they're not giving an inch. Maybe they want to make an impression on the Rangers, or whatever team they meet on Friday."

"Is this the same pitcher they used on Monday?"

"No, it's a different one, but he's using the same tactics. I don't think we should turn baseball into a sissy sport, but this isn't baseball, the way it looks to me."

"What is the other manager doing?"

"Nothing, I guess. He may have protested to the umpires, but he's not making a big stew about it, and they're not doing anything to stop it. Maybe he'll file a protest with the bigwigs after the game is over, and they'll probably take a month to consider. A fat lot of good that will do if somebody gets conked first. Thank goodness for plastic batting helmets, anyway."

"What would you do if you were the manager?"

"Tell my pitcher to fire back at them, I suppose," Nelson answered.

"And where do you think that would end?"

"I don't know," said Nelson grimly, "but at least I'd be sure where it began."

The game wore on to a close. The Bobtails never rallied. It was impossible to tell whether they were demoralized, or simply outclassed. Even Nelson had to admit that the Bearcats had a good team.

"Well, what's with you, Ted?" he asked, as he began to pack up.

"If I thought I had a thousand and one things to do to begin with, now it's doubled or tripled. It seems the old things never get finished, and the new ones keep piling up. It's hard to know where to turn."

"Do the important things first," advised Nelson. "That's what you said."

"I know that's what I said. But while I'm attending to everything else, I get the feeling I'm neglecting the most important thing of all—finding out what Ken Kutler is up to."

12 Not a Threat but a Promise

At one o'clock Ted and Nelson were in the office of the *Town Crier,* looking over the prints Nelson had ready, and consulting with Mr. Dobson about them. Though the editor had the final decisions to make, for the most part he was ready to accept Ted's judgment. Occasionally he had to point out to Ted that a certain combination or procedure would cause difficulties in making up the page, but otherwise the four-page baseball section was to be printed the way Ted planned it. He had never had a responsibility quite like this one before, and he was eager to show what he could do.

It was short notice, of course, since Mr. Dobson had only announced his decision the previous day. But Ted had expected that there would be at least two pages of baseball material, and had planned to prepare even more than this to be certain of having enough, so the decision did not leave him completely unprepared.

"Although it's a shame we couldn't have the special section next Tuesday instead," he announced. "Then we could cover the entire tournament."

"I'm afraid the excitement will have pretty well died down by that time, Ted. That would be four days after the tournament was over. This way our Friday morning edition will come out while the teams are going into the finals and excitement is at its peak."

"And while it's true that you won't be covering the complete tournament, Ted," Nelson interposed, "you'll have a good deal of it by anticipation. You won't have the final scores, but people like to read about a sporting event before it happens just about as much as they do afterward. Besides, we'll be having some pictures of the winning teams, even though we don't know now how everything will come out."

"I wish we could have a picture for *every* team," said Ted a little wistfully.

But Nelson snorted. He knew less about newspaper work than the others, but he did know pictures. "And make it look like a rogues' gallery? That's about the dullest set of pictures you could imagine—especially if you try to get in everybody on the team standing or sitting in a row. Actually, it's the quality of the pictures, rather than who happens to be in them that's the most important in this work. Maybe the players wouldn't agree, but we're concerned with the general readers."

"Nelson does have a point," Mr. Dobson agreed. He picked up a few of the prints. "But I don't think we're going to have to apologize for these pictures, Nelson. Rather, our problem will be one of selection. Here you've really caught something."

He held up a picture in which Nelson had snapped a player gaping in shocked surprise as the umpire called him out on strikes.

"I'm glad you like it," said Nelson modestly. "This team was badly defeated in the first round. But it's just as I said to Ted—the picture is more important than the team."

The discussion continued for some time as they looked over Nelson's pictures while he told them what he had at home but not yet printed, and what he expected to get. Meanwhile Ted was busy blocking out the pages, deciding how to arrange the pictures and how much text to write to go with them.

"How are you going to describe the baseball games?" asked Nelson. "You haven't seen them all."

"No, but I have a carbon copy of every score sheet, and I think that at least we can print the final score and a short description of every game. And then, on those games I haven't seen, I've tried to talk with someone who did see them, and I've made notes on the high points. In every baseball game there's the moment of highest tension when the result could still go either way, and after that the excitement dies down. But the funny thing is you can't always recognize that peak just by looking at the box score. You have to be there to know. So I'm taking notes on all the outstanding plays in the game, and trying to describe the peaks from them."

"Will you have any trouble finishing in time?" Mr. Dobson questioned.

"No, I don't think so, but I'll have to skip the Rangers' game."

"Isn't that what you wanted to see most, Ted?" asked Nelson.

"I'd like to see it, but you can't have everything. Look at poor Cliff—probably busy moving cots out of the gym."

"Huh, if I know Cliff he's probably sleeping on them instead of moving them," said Nelson, snorting.

They were about to leave the office when Mr. Sinclair, the manager of the Rangers, came in. They all knew and respected him.

"Mr. Dobson," he began, "and you, too, Ted, and Nelson—I guess I might just as well say this in front of all of you. I noticed you boys at the Bearcats' game this morning. What did you think of it?"

"They're a pretty good team," Nelson remarked. "Were you referring to the pitcher's poor control?"

"You can call it that, if you want to. I don't see it that way. When you can *predict* the next pitch is coming close to the batter, then I no longer believe it's a matter of poor control. What's your opinion, Ted?"

"Well, I thought there was something more than poor control involved."

"Was any protest made?" Mr. Dobson inquired.

"Yes, I happen to know that the manager of the Bobtails talked quietly with the umpires between innings. He didn't storm out on the field, but he was doing his best to get the matter adjusted. But he never got to first base. The umpires stated that in their opinion the pitcher was simply brushing back the players, keeping them from standing too close to the plate or from digging in. They couldn't see that that involved a violation of the rules, and they pointed out that no one was actually hit with a pitched ball. Well, in my opinion, when that happens it might be just one pitch too late.

"Now, you are aware from the schedule that if the Rangers win their game today, then we'll be facing the Bearcats on Friday. If we do, it is quite possible that they will use the same tactics. It is even possible that the same team of umpires will be in charge, so that a protest will be useless. I want to put myself on record right now: if such a thing happens I will immediately take my team off the field."

The others sat and stood in shocked silence, hardly prepared for such a development as this. The Forestdale team had played hard all season. If it got into the finals, that meant it had survived its preliminary tests. After having aroused all these high hopes, it seemed unthinkable that the Rangers were to lose their last game on a forfeit. Yet it was hard for them to say that Mr. Sinclair was not acting within his rights unless there was a suitable alternative open to him. He was a reputable, sincere man, and undoubtedly he would do exactly as he thought right.

"Had you thought of registering a protest with the baseball committee?" asked Mr. Dobson.

"Yes, I have, but it might take them too long to make up their minds. Besides, I don't want to be placed in the position of complaining before I have a personal grievance, nor do I want to appear to be a chronic complainer. You people know that I'm not that."

"Do you intend to talk with Mr. Wyatt first?" Mr. Dobson inquired.

"No, I do not. That is another step I had considered. But judging by the type of man he is, this just might get his back up. He might feel that I had challenged him, and that he had to go through with it even when, perhaps, he might not otherwise have done so. I don't want to give him any excuse. Let the decision be clearly his."

"A great many people would be disappointed if you forfeited the game," the editor pointed out.

"I know that—and none of them more than the players on our team, the very boys I am trying to protect. But if we saw the boys throwing bricks at each other, we'd stop it. Well, a baseball is similar to a brick, with the corners rounded off. If Abner Doubleday had wanted it to be that kind of game, he would have invented a different set of rules. So the only way to stop it is to bring the matter out into the open."

"Are your pitchers under orders not to come too close to the opposing batters?" asked Ted.

"They're under orders not to hit another player deliberately, or to make him dodge the ball deliberately. Naturally there are bound to be accidents in any sport. Players are running, there are collisions and falls, bats and balls and spikes form weapons of a sort. But I want to be sure that whatever happens is an accident. Then at least it's not a matter of conscience."

"You wouldn't let your pitcher fire at the other batters, even when their pitcher is doing it to you?" Nelson put in.

"Then least of all. Let the blame fall clearly on the other side. If my boys get involved, too, then before long it will be difficult to say who started it and who kept it going. They will be just as much to blame as the others."

"I see a difficulty here," Mr. Dobson interposed, "in that boys have a natural tendency to imitate the major league stars they admire. Apparently a good deal of this sort of thing does go on in the major leagues."

"But even the major leagues don't approve of the bean ball," Nelson was quick to point out. "The umpires often warn a pitcher, and he faces a fine and possible suspension."

"Yes," Mr. Sinclair agreed, "but they go rather far in tolerating the brush-back pitch, merely designed to keep the batter loose, as they call it. That they miss the batter is no credit to them. I'm not here to criticize the major leagues. They have their own set of problems. The players are professionals, confident of their ability to take care of themselves, with their own methods of enforcement, their own channels of appeal. If things get too bad, the rules can be changed.

"We have a different situation here. I'm quite certain that the responsibility I feel toward the boys on my team is different from that which a major league manager feels toward his players.

"So, I repeat, I won't allow my boys to go through the kind of game I saw going on at Eastgate this morning. If I see a bean ball, then they will leave the field. That's not a threat—it's a promise. And it won't take two balls to convince me."

"Would you like me to talk with Mr. Wyatt?" asked Mr. Dobson.

"I wouldn't presume to tell you what to do, Mr. Dobson. I just wanted to be certain that my own position was clear."

As no one had anything to suggest, Mr. Sinclair said goodbye and left. Finally Ted said:

"Is leaving the field—forfeiting the game—letting the Bearcats have their victory without even putting up a fight—is that the best way to handle the matter?"

"Mr. Sinclair thinks it is, unless we can show him a better way. I'll put it up to you—if you had a boy playing on a team, would you rather have Mr. Sinclair or Mr. Wyatt acting as manager?"

"Mr. Sinclair, without a doubt," Ted replied.

"Yes," Nelson agreed, "but the boy himself might prefer to play under Mr. Wyatt. You can't argue with success."

"Maybe that's the key to the problem. Mr. Wyatt is successful. Then the answer is to try to make his kind of tactics unsuccessful. I admit I don't know how to go about it. A little newspaper publicity might help, but it would be too late to do any good in this particular tournament." Mr. Dobson got up from his desk. "Ted. I have to run over to the bank for a few minutes. Will you stay in charge of the office till I get back? I hate to make you late for the baseball game, but Nelson can go on ahead if he wants to, and you can use my car when I get back."

"I guess I may as well wait, too," Nelson responded. "It won't hurt if I don't get there exactly at the beginning of the game."

"We need pictures," Ted reminded him.

"I know, but I'm getting tired of posed pictures, the kind I'd get before the game. I'm after some good action shots."

Mr. Dobson left and Ted picked up some papers to look over while Nelson gave his attention to his pictures.

"I just wish there was some way for us to fix Mr. Wyatt's wagon," Nelson remarked. "If only those Bobtails had been able to beat him, then we would have been rid of him. But I guess the Bearcats were just too good for them."

"I'd like to do something about him, too," said Ted with a sigh. "But after all, we've got to be reasonable. Mr. Wyatt is a loudmouth, but I guess there's no law against that. And he may be ordering his pitchers to throw at batters, but the umpires think he's acting within the letter of the rules, and they're the ones who have the say. And that's really all I've got against him. You can't criticize a man just because he drives a flashy sports car–"

Nelson looked up at him, incredulous. "Ted, I always knew the heat would get you and now you've really flipped. He drives a green convertible. I saw it the other night after the game. What would he be doing with a sports car here? He's got to haul players and equipment–what good is a sports car for that?"

It was Ted's turn to be confused. He was quite certain that he had seen Mr. Wyatt get into a two-toned brown sports job after talking with him at the office. Yet he had a feeling that Nelson was right, too. Certainly a bigger car would be much better for the purpose of getting players to the touroment. It would, in fact, take at least two and more likely three cars to get a team to Forestdale—but it was hardly likely a sports car would be one of them.

Before he could quite figure it out, Margaret Lake opened the door and put her head in.

"Ted, there's a telephone call for you over here. A Mr. Saunders. He said it was important so I thought I'd better call you."

"I'll hold down the fort." Nelson waved Ted on.

Next door, Ted picked up the phone. "Hello, Mr. Saunders?"

"Ted? When I said it was important, I meant it was important to me. I wonder if you could do me a favor. I'd like to look over the box scores for the touroment games so far, and I understand you have copies."

"Yes, I do—that is, I have just one copy for each game. I couldn't let you take them out, but I guess it would be all right if you looked them over here."

"I'll do that, Ted. I'll be right over, and thanks."

Ted gave instructions to Margaret to allow Mr. Saunders to look over the sheets when he came in, then returned to the newspaper office where he explained his errand to Nelson.

He raised his eyebrows. "Do you think that was wise, Ted?"

"What do you mean?"

"Mr. Saunders might be a gambler, you know, instead of a real scout. He might be anxious to get this information out so he can quote the latest gambling odds in plenty of time for his organization."

"Sure, and he might be a real scout, anxious to get a line on some player before anyone else does. A man's innocent until proven guilty."

"Is that in the Bill of Rights?"

"The spirit of the thing is there, but you have to think about it."

Then Mr. Dobson returned, and the boys were off for Westgate in Nelson's car.

13   A Grudge

When they arrived at the field, they found that the first inning was already over, and the Eaglets were leading the Typhoons, two to nothing. The stands were crowded, and the only place Ted could find to sit was on the ground in front of the first row of the grandstand. Nelson, with his camera ready, went directly out on the field to the photographer's circle. Here he had a good focus on the pitcher or home plate, and possibly, by swiveling quickly, first base. A play at one of the other bases would require a longer shot. He even intended to try a few pictures of the outfield, switching quickly to a telephoto lens, but he knew that his results here would be uncertain.

Ted's first thought was whether Larry and Cal had got into the game. He had no scorecard or lineup, and the pitcher on the mound certainly didn't look like Larry, but was probably the same pitcher they had used on Monday. Then he spotted his friends out in the bullpen, and knew that again they hadn't made it. Cal, in fact, was warming up two pitchers, Larry and someone else Ted did not know.

Ted knew that these teams were on the spot in regard to their pitching. Usually playing only two games a week, they ordinarily depended for the most part upon one star pitcher. But with possibly three games coming this week, they had to look to other resources. The Bearcats, that morning, had turned to a second pitcher, who apparently was about as good as the first and he had been able to carry them. The Eaglets were less fortunate. They had started their star pitcher, Jan Allaine, on Monday and he had won. Mr. Ingram would un-

101

doubtedly have liked to rest him until Friday, but could he afford to do so? If the Eaglets lost today, there wouldn't be any game for them on Friday. So their manager, apparently lacking faith in the quality of his second-line pitchers, had started Jan with only one day of rest, hoping that his arm would hold up, or that he might at least get through a substantial part of the game.

It struck Ted immediately that if Jan was their star pitcher, he was below par on that particular day. He was in trouble almost as soon as the second inning started. The runner, having walked, was sacrificed to second, although Ted had his doubts it was a true sacrifice—the batter had hopes of beating it out. A long fly to center field, which was caught, then followed. But the next batter singled home the run. Another walk came next, but Jan put out the fire by striking out the batter who missed with three healthy swings.

It was possible that the Typhoons' pitcher was also suffering from insufficient rest, for he walked two in the last half of the inning, though no runs resulted. Ted could see where a team such as the Bearcats, which had two good pitchers, was entitled to some advantage over a team with only one good pitcher. But he could also see that a tired pitcher up against a fresh pitcher was going to suffer from a serious handicap. In this game there were apparently two tired pitchers, so it was hard to see where the advantage lay.

Jan was in trouble again in the third, but got out of it with a brilliant stop by the third baseman, the captain of the team, on a hard smash. Then the Eaglets scored an insurance run on a home run by the same captain in the last half of the third.

Nelson, finding himself out of film, returned to his car and obtained a fresh supply, then came to sit beside Ted for a minute while he reloaded his camera.

"I don't think Jan's going to make it, do you?"

"It doesn't look like it," Ted responded. "But I'm not sure

the other pitcher is going to make it, either. How is Jan usually? You saw him the other day."

"I learned that his reputation was very good, but I didn't think he had too much on the ball. He seemed to be in trouble most of the way in that game, too. Can't blame him much—it's been a long season, and the weight of it has been resting on his shoulders. It's just too much to expect one pitcher to do it all. Want to hear a piece of gossip?"

"Anything I can use in the paper?"

"I don't think you'd want to use it, but it's interesting just the same. I hear that Jan Allaine and Simon Hartrack are mortal enemies. They don't even talk to each other off the field. The captain—that's Eddie Youngman on third—told me that he's tried his best to patch things up, but there's something about them that rubs the other person the wrong way."

"Doesn't that hurt the team?"

"You'd think it might, but apparently not. They both try their best, just for the purpose of showing each other up. Anyway, they've had a pretty successful season."

"What's Mr. Ingram got to say about it?"

"According to Eddie, he finally decided he'd better let them alone. They're all right during the games, and he can't do very much about their conduct off the field. Nobody quite knows what happened, though, because they used to be real buddies. Suddenly—whiff. Neither one will say anything, but that's it."

"Odd. You wouldn't think they could keep up a grudge like that for very long, working as a battery the way they do. How long has this been going on?"

"Over a year, I guess. That's a long time for a kid to stay mad. Mr. Ingram assigned them to room together on this trip, thinking that might help, but it seems that it hasn't."

Now that Nelson had called the matter to his attention, Ted could see there was something in it. Their consultations out on the mound were brief and to the point, and never ended with

Simon giving his partner a slap on the back. They did what they had to do, and that was it. It was a puzzling situation to Ted. He couldn't see that it was much fun to play baseball this way, and if it wasn't fun for them, why were they playing? And what kind of grudge was it that had such a hold on them that a simple apology wouldn't cure?

Jan gave up another run in the top of the fourth, making the score three to two. Then the Eaglets threatened again, filling the bases with only one out. The catcher, Simon Hartrack, now came up to the plate. He was one of the team's big guns, as Ted had learned by now. If he could do no more than get out a long fly, he would at least hit in a run. Nelson was down near the foul line, his camera poised on the batter.

The first pitch was a called strike. It didn't seem to have much on it, Ted thought, but it was a difficult thing to judge from the seats. Besides, Simon may simply have been waiting the pitcher out.

The next pitch was also a called strike. Simon shook his head, as though in disagreement, and then stepped out of the box and looked around, as though uncertain what to do next. To Ted it seemed he had little choice. He couldn't afford another called strike, but would have to swing at anything that looked good.

He stepped back into the box. The pitcher took a long time getting the signal, then pitched from a windup, figuring that the runner on third wouldn't dare attempt a steal anyway. The pitch came in, not a fast ball, and seemingly not much of a curve, either. Expecting a blazer, Simon seemed to have been caught off stride and lunged at it, missing completely. He retreated to the bench. The next batter also made an out, and the Eaglets failed to score.

There had been no activity in the Eaglet bullpen for a little while, but now the two pitchers and the catcher were sent out to work again. Apparently Mr. Ingram did not feel he could go much farther with a very tired Jan. It occurred to Ted that the pitcher and the catcher were both trying too hard, and that may have been responsible for their failures. A feud could hurt a team in more ways than one.

Jan managed to stagger through the fifth inning, but when he came in and Mr. Ingram patted him on the back, Ted knew that the manager had had enough. A pinch hitter was sent up for him, and reached first on an error, but failed to score, as the rest of the batters were quickly retired.

Who would get the pitching nod? Ted hoped it would be his friend Larry, who had a chance to save the game if he could hold that one-run lead. Mr. Ingram beckoned to the bullpen, but it wasn't Larry who came. Apparently Larry was third-string, rather than second-string.

The new pitcher, whose name Ted did not know, didn't have Jan's ability but at least he was fresh. He retired the side, with only one runner reaching first base on a hit after two were out.

Then the Typhoons' pitcher also found his luck running out, and was soon deep in trouble. An error in the infield hurt him, but a triple along the left-field foul line hurt him even more. That runner scored on a single, and the following batter walked. That was enough, and a new pitcher came in. He was greeted with a bunt which advanced the runners. The next batter, the captain, then got out the long sacrifice fly which Simon had been unable to get earlier, and the third run was in. The Eaglets took a four-run lead into the seventh and last inning.

Alas, their pitcher found more trouble awaiting him. Not really fast, he seemed to be hunting for the corners of the plate with his curve and not finding them. The first batter walked. The second batter took three balls and then laid into a cripple for a single, advancing the runner to second. With a four-run lead, no one was looking for the bunt, which may have been the reason that the batter tried it. It was a good bunt, but in the catcher's territory. Simon ran out to field it, then made a perfect throw to second base—but no one was there to take it. The infield had been expecting the play to go to first, and the ball went through to the outfield. One runner scored easily, and the other slid into home just under the throw while the batter stopped at second.

Simon's disgust was obvious, but it was hard to say what should have been done. It was true that the sure out was more important than the extra base for the runner going to second. But had the shortstop been alert and taken the throw, there would have been runners on first and third with one out, and the stage would still have been set for a double play which might have gotten the pitcher out of further trouble. As though to prove the truth of this speculation, the next batter hit an easy grounder which would probably have been a double-play ball had the runner still been on first. Instead only one out could be made as the runner went to third.

The next batter struck out. Two away, and a two-run lead. A home run could tie it up, but the Eaglets were all right if they could only get this man. Simon ran out to talk to his pitcher, and ended by patting him on the back and running back to the plate. Whatever they had cooked up between them seemed to work, for the batter took one ball, then popped weakly to the infield. The Eaglets had done it, but the hard way.

Nelson was out trying to get pictures, but the Eaglets did not appear exactly a boisterous bunch. Perhaps they were tired, for the game had been long and full of tension. They shook hands with the pitcher, then walked slowly off the field. The pitcher paused, at Nelson's request, to allow his picture to be taken, then he followed his teammates to the bench and to the waiting cars.

"Either that's the coolest bunch of kids I ever saw," Nelson decided, packing up his equipment, "or else they're all pretty much down in the mouth. I never saw a team look so unhappy after winning a big game. Even if it was tight, you'd think that would make them feel all the more excited."

"Maybe that feud between the pitcher and the catcher is telling on them," Ted observed.

"Could be, or maybe they're thinking ahead to Friday. It looks to me like they've got big troubles. They had to use Jan today, and he didn't have much on the ball. The pitcher who followed him was no better than he had to be. Now Mr. Ingram will have to decide whether to use a very tired Jan on Friday, or turn to a second-stringer. Do you think this tournament really is fair, Ted, or does it impose too hard a burden on the pitchers in a short space of time?"

"Fair as it can be, I suppose. Apparently the Bearcats have two good starting pitchers, so I don't see that Mr. Wyatt, at least, has any real complaint."

"And the Rangers have only one. That could lead to trouble. You still aren't going to the Rangers' game, Ted?"

Ted shook his head. "I can't squeeze it in, with that special section due at the printer's by noon tomorrow. I've got hours and hours of writing to do. What's on your schedule?"

"Get home and do a little work on my pictures, I guess, and then get over to Eastgate for the Rangers' game. I'll try to keep you posted, Ted."

Ted went to work at the office, unhappily aware that he was missing the excitement out at Eastgate, but there was no help for it. He also learned that the Young'uns had lost their game at Eastgate and had already left town. He made good progress with his work, so that the four pages were beginning to take final shape in his mind. A telephone call came in from Jim who said that he was calling at Nelson's orders, and the Rangers were ahead, three to nothing, at the end of three innings. Nelson also claimed to have taken a couple of good pictures which he was sure would interest Ted. Ted thought they would if they were any good at all. *Town Crier* readers would probably be more interested in their own team than in the others.

He received another call at the end of six innings. The

Rangers were still ahead, this time by a score of seven to five, though they had been behind for a time. It sounded like a wild contest. And then as the game ended, Nelson put in an appearance as Ted could see the crowds streaming home from the field.

"Well, we won," Nelson announced gloomily.

"Why so cheerful about it?"

"Because Mr. Sinclair had to use Murdock after all. He came in in relief in the fourth inning, and pitched more than half the game. I guess we were all hoping Murdock would be able to go fresh into the game Friday with the Bearcats. But the way things were going, the game might have gone right down the drain today without Murdock. Mr. Sinclair really didn't have much choice."

Ted pointed out, "Just a few hours ago you couldn't understand why the Eaglets were gloomy after winning, and now you're the same way."

Nelson could manage no more than half a smile. "I guess it's a little different, when it's your own team. No fooling, Ted, I think the Rangers have got more than a handful. They had a fairly easy opponent today, and just managed to squeeze it out, ten to nine. Those Bearcats are good, and their star pitcher is fresh, while Murdock is tired. I just hope we don't get slaughtered."

"We may lose by nine runs, you know," Ted reminded him.

"How do you figure that?"

"A forfeit—if Mr. Sinclair takes his team off the field."

"That's right, Ted. I forgot about that for the moment. And I'm not doubting for a single minute that that's exactly what Mr. Sinclair will do if he sees his duty that way. Isn't there anything we can do about it, Ted?"

"I can't think of anything."

They left for home together where Ted found his mother holding a late supper for him. Larry and Cal were there in a subdued mood. Ted tried to talk to them about their game, and found that they weren't much interested. It was hard to tell whether it was the feud that bothered them, or worry over the next game, or simply pique over their failure to get into today's game. After all, Larry may have had good reason to feel that he would get the nod after Jan Allaine had been lifted. Cal may have been upset by a slight to his buddy, or he might have had hopes of getting in himself as Larry's catcher.

Upon being asked, they said they had no plans for the evening. Apparently they had seen the Rangers' game, or part of it, but they didn't feel like talking about that, either. Finally they said they would watch a little television and get to bed early. Ted wondered if they intended to sulk all day tomorrow.

He walked back to the office, and put in several more hours of work there, looking in at the baseball headquarters a few times to straighten out matters. Margaret told him that Mr. Saunders had stopped in as he had promised, and looked over all the scores. It had been Margaret's impression that he had been interested in only one of the score sheets, but that he looked at all of them in order to prevent her from knowing which one.

Late in the evening, Nelson came down to the office to join Ted, bringing more pictures, and they discussed selections. As Nelson had promised, he did have some good shots of the games that day. Then Nelson drove Ted home, where Ted found his guests already in bed.

"Did they seem in any better spirits?" he asked his mother.

"I don't think so. They hardly said a word all evening, except for a polite good-night when they went upstairs."

"Do you think they were mad at each other?"

"No, I don't think so. It looked more like the two of them against the whole world."

When Ted got to bed, he stayed awake reviewing the events of a busy day. Suddenly he recalled that he and Nelson had had a dispute over what kind of car Mr. Wyatt drove, but had not settled it. It seemed silly to worry over such a trifle now, and he finally fell asleep.

14 Absent without Leave

Afterward Ted could not tell what it was that awakened him. It must have been a noise of some sort. It was beginning to grow light outside. He looked at the clock. It was a little after six so his alarm was not due to go off for another hour yet, and his visitors could sleep still later if they wished. He wanted to put his head back on the pillow and fall asleep again, but some nagging worry forced him to get up and go quietly downstairs. He found that the front door was unlocked, though he knew it had been locked the night before.

He went back upstairs and tapped lightly on the door of the guest room. There was no response. Then he pushed the door open. Cal was alone in the room. At first Ted supposed that he was merely pretending to sleep. He went over to the bed and shook him by the shoulder. But the boy awakened, and seemed genuinely puzzled to find Ted there and Larry missing.

"What's going on here?" Ted asked quietly but firmly.

"I–I don't know," said Cal in seeming puzzlement.

"Where is Larry?"

"I don't know," said Cal, shaking his head. "He went home, I suppose. Where else would he go?"

"Did you know he was going?"

"No," said Cal bitterly. "If I'd known it, I would have gone with him!"

"Did he have enough money for busfare?"

"I guess so. I don't know for sure."

Ted sat down on the chair beside the bed. "Look, I don't have time to go into this whole situation with you now–not if I'm going to have any chance of finding Larry. Will you promise me one thing—that you won't leave here until I come back and have had a chance to talk with you?"

Cal seemed to consider this matter for a long time. "All right, I won't leave, until you get back."

With this promise to go on, Ted returned to his room to dress, and hurriedly left the house.

Where to now? The bus depot was the most obvious place to look, but somehow Ted had a feeling that this wasn't the answer. Larry would certainly be very conspicuous in the nearly deserted station. There was an eleven P.M. curfew, and no one had said how long it extended into the morning hours, but Ted felt sure that if Larry were spotted by the police at that hour, they would stop and question him.

No, Larry would probably want to get out of town as quickly as possible. Perhaps he hoped to hitchhike a ride, for Cal could have been wrong about his having enough money, or he might have hoped that a ride would throw pursuers off the trail. During this baseball tournament, drivers were being more tolerant about picking up boys along the road, knowing that some of them were rooming at motels some distance outside of town. But hardly any driver would pick up a boy at such an early hour.

Larry lived to the south, and if he were headed home he was probably bound for the southern boundary of the town, hoping to avoid the police and get there in time to pick up a ride from some early driver. But would he be going home? Somehow Ted had the impression that Larry didn't want to talk with anyone, which might mean that he wasn't anxious to talk with his parents, either. Then what were his plans? Trying to put himself into Larry's place, Ted decided that for some reason the pitcher wanted to jump the team. Though he would like to go home, his early arrival there would touch off questions, so probably he simply intended to wander around until the tournament was over, and then go home just as though everything was all right. Possibly his parents were not intimate enough either with Mr. Ingram or some of the other boys and their parents to ask questions, but would accept his return as a matter of course.

There were objections to this theory, of course. As soon as Mr. Ingram missed Larry, he would probably notify his parents, and they in turn might decide that the police should be notified, in which case he was likely to be picked up soon. But these were consequences which Larry might not have fully thought through.

If Ted's theory were right then Larry was probably standing at that very moment at the crest of Holly Hill, since he could not hope to get a ride on the slope itself, trying to thumb a ride *away* from home.

Since Larry had had a head start on him, the first thing Ted would need was a car. Mr. Dobson would not be at the office yet, and the only other car available was Nelson's. Ted quickly walked the few blocks to Nelson's home. Either the telephone or the doorbell was likely to arouse some other member of the household long before it did Nelson, who was not noted for his early rising. Ted could think of nothing better than the old-fashioned device of picking up a few pebbles and tossing them up against Nelson's bedroom window. He was successful, and Nelson's face soon appeared at the screen.

"I need a car–quick."

"OK. You want me, too?"

"No, just the keys."

Nelson disappeared from the window for a moment, then reappeared, opened the screen, and tossed down a ring of keys. He wasn't going to ask any leading questions just then, knowing that their voices might be overhead, but he did yawn and say:

"What day is it?"

"Thursday," and Ted went off to get the car.

He was soon on his way. As he started to climb Holly Hill, he saw a boy standing near the road, obviously seeking a ride.

It was Larry. Ted felt pleased that he had been able to put himself into Larry's place to this extent. But he still did not know the reason for Larry's behavior. Quite clearly something had happened at yesterday's game, for before the game Larry and Cal had been bubbling over with enthusiasm, while afterward they were glum and taciturn in spite of their team's victory. Ted and Nelson had seen most of the game, but had noticed nothing wrong. Could the boys have been mad about not getting into the game? But Ted recalled that Larry had told him on Sunday he hoped he *wouldn't* get into a game, because this would mean the starting pitcher was off. It might have been a personal insult, but Ted didn't feel that Larry was particularly sensitive in this way, and anyway whatever happened had affected Cal just as much.

He drew to a stop at the top of the hill and threw open the door. Larry hopped into the car, for the moment recognizing neither the car nor Ted. But it was only a matter of seconds before he realized what had happened, and he slumped back into his seat.

"Where are we going?" he asked.

"There's an all-night diner about a mile and a half up ahead. Let's stop off and get some breakfast. I don't think either of us can do our best thinking on an empty stomach. Anyway, this is the direction you wanted to go."

Larry made no reply, which Ted took for consent, and they drove on. No further words were exchanged between them until they had reached the diner and gone inside. Ted looked over the menu, entered his own order, and asked:

"The same for you, Larry?"

"OK," Larry agreed, without enthusiasm.

But upset as he was, Larry's naturally healthy appetite came to the fore, and he ate a good breakfast. Finally they were both finished.

"Now where do we go?" Larry demanded.

"Anywhere you want to go. I'm at your service."

"Don't you have work to do?"

"You can say that twice. I've got that special four-page base-ball section due by noon, plus all my regular chores at both offices. But first things first."

"Am I a first thing?"

"Yes," said Ted firmly.

"Are you a newspaper reporter now?"

"No, I'm still your host–and your friend, I hope. Look, Larry, I know you don't want to talk to Mr. Ingram, and it would seem that you don't want to talk to your parents, either. I have even less right to your confidence than they have, but I am closer to your age, and may be a little better able to see things your way. Is there anything you want to talk to me about?"

Larry shook his head.

"All right, then, Larry, I don't want to pry. But may I ask just one question? Are you being chased by a bear?"

Larry looked up. "I don't understand."

"If you were being chased by a bear, I think running away might be the best thing–maybe the only thing–for you to do. Is this that kind of problem, or is it the other kind of prob-lem that goes right on being a problem whether you're there or not?"

"I guess it's the other kind of problem," Larry admitted.

"The kind of problem that might even get worse, if you're not there to help?"

"I guess so," said Larry slowly.

"Well, then, Larry, where do we go from here?"

"I guess, maybe, it would be better to go back." Larry was blinking hard. "If I go back, may we stay at your house all day?"

Then Ted understood one more link in the puzzling chain. There was some person or persons whom the boys did not want to meet.

"Don't you want to see the baseball games today?"

"No."

"Or play in your game tomorrow?"

Larry considered. "No," he decided.

"All right, Larry, you can stay home today if you want to."

"And if Cal and I decide we want to leave tonight, you won't try to stop us?"

"No—but I will have to notify Mr. Ingram."

"After we're gone?"

"Yes, if that's the way you want it, and if you promise not to leave before this evening, and then go straight home."

"That's a bargain, Ted. We won't leave before evening, and if we do leave, we'll go straight home."

At his house, Ted explained matters briefly to his mother, then left for the newspaper office. This was the big morning for him. Mr. Dobson had to be consulted on the final layout. Nelson was there, being as helpful as he could. Final decisions were reached on the remaining pictures, and Ted wrote up the necessary captions and copy. Cliff and Jim were attending the two games in progress that morning, and phoned in their final reports at around eleven-thirty. Ted was able to include this information in the space he had saved for it. At shortly before twelve o'clock the complete four-page section had been assembled and approved, and was taken back to the printer.

"All right, Nel, let's get out of here," Ted suggested.

"Lunch?"

"Maybe, if we can find some quiet spot. Just now I want to get out from under."

They managed to find a diner some distance from town where they could talk in some privacy. Ted put through a call to his mother, explaining that he would not be home for lunch, and asking about the two boys.

"They've been carrying things up to the attic for me, Ted," she reported. "That doesn't seem a very polite way to treat guests, but they're eager to help. I don't know what the trouble is all about, Ted, but these are really nice boys."

Ted had given Nelson a brief account of his troubles with Larry during the morning rush, but now they were able to discuss the matter more fully.

"How do you figure it, Ted?"

"The only way I can see it is that these boys are in some state of confusion or doubt. It reminds me of the bean-ball situation with Mr. Wyatt. Mr. Sinclair is very certain about what's going on, but there's no way for him to prove it. Nevertheless, he is in a position to act if he feels he should. Larry and Cal may also be in a situation where they suspect something, but can't prove it, and they're in no position to do anything about it. So Larry lost his head for a moment, and thought that the easiest thing was for him to run away."

"Could this thing that's worrying them have anything to do with gambling, Ted?"

"It could, and of course that's the thing that's been on my mind, coming after Ken's tip. But if there is a big-time gambler here, is it Mr. Saunders, Mr. Scotch, or someone else?"

"I thought for a while it was Mr. Saunders, the way he was interested in seeing those box scores in such a hurry."

"Well, that hardly proves it. Certainly whatever he did was done openly, if that means anything."

"Not much." Nelson grunted. "Why shouldn't he do things openly, if he doesn't know you suspect him?"

"Wouldn't he have a guilty conscience?"

"If those guys have a conscience."

"I don't mean a conscience about being sorry, but a conscience about getting caught. I should think he would exercise every possible precaution."

"If it isn't Mr. Hill and isn't Mr. Saunders, then that leaves Mr. Scotch. But you can't prove anything against him that way, can you?"

"Not very well. Another thing on my mind is Mr. Wyatt, and that little discussion we had on the kind of car he drove."

Nelson looked surprised. "Does that have anything to do with our present problem, Ted?"

"Maybe not, but we've got more than one problem. If we can't do something about Mr. Wyatt, Mr. Sinclair is almost certain to blow the lid off tomorrow. He's in such a mood that if a pitch even looks as though it *might* be a bean ball, he'll pull the Rangers off the field. And just about the last thing you'd want, or I'd want, or almost anybody in Forestdale would want, is for the Bearcats to win on a forfeit."

"Well, OK, Ted, I don't quite see the point of it, but it shouldn't be a difficult matter to check up on that car. You'd know it if you saw it, wouldn't you?"

"Undoubtedly. It's probably the only one like it in Forestdale, and maybe even the county."

"Then the chances are good that the place to find it is in the hotel parking lot. Anyway we can go and check, and if it isn't there we can probably get some information from the attendant."

"Do you want to take any more pictures?" asked Ted, getting up from their table.

"No—what's the use? Mr. Dobson won't use more than one or two in next Tuesday's paper, and it would be better to have pictures from the finals tomorrow."

At the hotel parking lot they easily found the car that Ted claimed to have seen Mr. Wyatt driving. Nelson did not remember having seen it before, although it was a car he would certainly have remembered. He looked it over carefully, and while doing so noticed something on the ground, partly concealed by a fender. It was a notebook, and it had the name James Scotch on the cover.

"Mr. Scotch's notebook," he pointed out to Ted. "Then this is probably his car. Do we give him back his notebook?"

"Of course we do. It isn't ours."

"But do we look in it first? Remember we're interested in

finding out whether he's really a baseball scout or a gambler."

"If he's a scout, he may have some private information in there that's no business of ours. And if he's a gambler he's probably got his information so disguised that we wouldn't be able to make head or tail out of it."

Nelson grinned. "Then we won't look into his notebook. It's so easy to do right, when you know it won't cost you anything."

They took the notebook into the hotel and showed it to the desk clerk, also inquiring about the car in the parking lot.

"Yes, that's Mr. Scotch's car," the clerk assured them, "and I'll send up his notebook to him."

"Maybe we could take the notebook up ourselves," suggested Ted. "You might ask him on the telephone."

The clerk shook his head. "Not on the house telephone. He has given instructions not to put through any calls on it."

"You mean that he has another telephone?"

"Yes, a private telephone. We have rooms equipped with outside telephones, since some of our business customers sometimes request it."

"But you have the number of the telephone?"

"No, it's usually changed for each customer, and in this case Mr. Scotch requested an unlisted number."

"Well, then," said Ted, considering, "I guess we won't bother. Just send up the notebook with our thanks."

Nelson grumbled a little as they walked away from the desk. "He'll think we looked in it even when we didn't, and where does that leave us if there *is* something important in there? Don't you think he must be a gambler, Ted, with that private telephone?"

"Not necessarily. A baseball scout might want a private telephone, too. Whichever he is, Mr. Wyatt is apparently intimate enough with him to drive his car. It's possible Mr. Wyatt could be intimate with either a scout or a gambler, but I wish there was some way for us to figure out which it is."

15 On the Carpet

It was Nelson's suggestion that they go out to Westgate.

"I remember where Mr. Scotch was sitting to watch the game, and I'd like to see just what a scout would see at a game he was scouting–if he really is a scout."

"Wouldn't that depend on which player he was scouting?"

"Yes, and it might depend even more on where there happened to be a seat available. But let's try it, anyway."

They did, taking a place about halfway up in the low grandstand, and about halfway between home plate and first base. The stands were nearly empty, but there were players practicing down on the field, and others along the sidelines watching them.

"This is a good spot to watch the pitcher, catcher, third baseman and shortstop," Nelson decided, "and in these lower classifications that's all that matters. It's unusual to put a good man in the outfield or even on the right side of the infield except under special circumstances."

Ted agreed with a mumbled grunt, but other than that had little to say, his mind on other things.

"What's up, doc?" Nelson demanded.

"Just the same thing. Is Mr. Scotch a scout or a gambler? I'm trying to think back to that interview we had with him to see if I can remember anything that might have given him away."

"As I recall, he didn't have very much to say about anything."

"No, not until the question of Fred Ewer came up. Then he asked something about–" Ted suddenly brightened, sitting up very straight. "He asked a question about what fields Fred hit to, and you remember what you said?"

"Something about Fred's having been up against a right-handed pitcher when Mr. Scotch saw him."

"Sure—that's it! Mr. Scotch didn't even know that Fred was a switch hitter! Now if he were a scout, engaged in a race to get Fred's name down on a contract, wouldn't he know every last little detail about him?"

"Why—why sure, he would," Nelson agreed. "A gambler would be interested, too, but he would be mostly concerned with how good a player a boy was. He wouldn't have all this small information about everyone right at his fingertips."

"Then Mr. Scotch is a gambler, and Mr. Wyatt has been in touch with him. I think that's a piece of information we ought to lay in front of Mr. Dobson."

At the *Town Crier* office, the editor listened to their story carefully. Then he reached for the telephone.

"Are you going to ask Mr. Wyatt to come down here?" Ted questioned.

"No, I have no authority to put him on the carpet. But I'm going to call someone who does—Mr. Jarvis, head of the baseball committee."

The call was put through, and Mr. Jarvis said he would be right over. When he arrived, Mr. Dobson explained the situation to him, and the baseball chairman considered it thoughtfully.

"Well, you certainly have gotten together a case. Of course there is a chance that you are completely wrong, in which event Mr. Wyatt will no doubt be quite happy to explain the matter to us. At least he is entitled to a chance to explain." He put through a call to Mr. Wyatt, asking the Bearcats' manager to come down to the newspaper office, and apparently got his consent. "Don't leave, boys," Mr. Jarvis went on, after hanging up the phone. "If you are making an accusation against a man, the least you can do is to have the courage to face him."

"Oh, I wasn't leaving," said Nelson, seating himself comfortably in an office chair.

Mr. Wyatt soon put in an appearance, seemingly surprised to find such a group waiting for him. Mr. Jarvis asked him to sit down.

"Mr. Wyatt, some information has come to me which may or may not be true, and which you may or may not already know about. My information is that a man named James Scotch, now registered at the Forestdale Hotel, may be a gambler, although he is ostensibly appearing here as a baseball scout. Do you have any information about that?"

"Offhand, I would say no," said Mr. Wyatt sharply.

"Another piece of information that has come to me," Mr. Jarvis went on smoothly, "is that you have been seen driving Mr. Scotch's car."

"Well, what if I have? I didn't know that was illegal. If there was anything wrong about it, would I have been doing it openly?"

"It would hardly appear to be illegal, Mr. Wyatt, but it does bring up some question about your relationship to the man. If there is any explanation you would care to offer about Mr. Scotch, or about your association with him, we would like to hear it."

Mr. Wyatt stared at the group, "I don't think I have to explain either Mr. Scotch or my association with him," he said angrily. "I will associate with anyone I please. I have done nothing at all criminal, and unless you can prove that I have, I don't see that you have any right to ask me for an explanation."

"If you have engaged in gambling activities, Mr. Wyatt, I have every right to ask for an explanation. Am I to understand that you deny such activities?"

The baseball manager hesitated. He didn't know, of course,

what information Mr. Jarvis possessed, and began to fear this information might be of a more damaging nature than the truth.

"All right, then, I'll tell you. I placed a bet with him on my *own* team. That will show you how much confidence I have in them. I don't see how you can find any fault with such a transaction. It's done every day in the racing world."

"But this is the world of amateur baseball, Mr. Wyatt. I take it this was a fairly sizable wager?"

"Sizable enough, I would say. I'm no penny pincher."

"A man who has made a wager on his own team might be especially concerned over winning or losing, and this would be likely to communicate itself to the players. It might also make him blame his players if they should fail. This is an element that we would prefer not to inject into our games, Mr. Wyatt. Other actions of yours have already come to our attention—"

"You're referring to our use of the brush-back pitch, of course. Let me tell you that I've simply been teaching our boys to stand up for themselves and fight for their place in the world. It's what they would have to do if they went on into major league baseball or if they turned to some other adult pursuit."

"Of course, Mr. Wyatt, it is difficult to know just where to draw the line with respect to the brush-back pitch, but I don't think there is any question about where to draw the line on this other matter. We prefer our games to be free of even a suspicion of betting for financial gain. Therefore, I am asking you to withdraw as manager of the Bearcats, and turn the team over to your assistant."

"I'm not even to be given the benefit of a hearing, I suppose?"

"Oh, yes, you may have a hearing before the full baseball committee any time you request it."

"Much good it would do. I know how you hold the committee in the hollow of your hand." He turned upon Ted with a sneer. "I suppose I have you to thank for this."

"No, Mr. Wyatt," said Mr. Jarvis quietly, "you have *yourself* to thank."

Mr. Wyatt looked at them for a moment, then turned and strode violently out of the office.

"I'd like to thank you, Ted," said Mr. Jarvis. "It took a very observing person to notice that Mr. Wyatt was driving someone else's car. It was his vanity in driving this very expensive car that led to his discovery."

"Oh, anyone could have done that," Ted protested.

"Sure," Nelson agreed, "but it took Ted to make the logical deduction from it. This kid's a real brain," he added in spite of Ted's frown.

A few minutes later, after Mr. Jarvis had left, Ted had partly forgiven him. "Let's go for a little ride," he requested.

"To cool off?" asked Nelson.

"No, I want to think. But before I start thinking, I wish you'd drop me off at the hotel. I want to see someone."

"Not Mr. Scotch?"

"No, someone else," but Ted did not offer to name the person.

"Well, the least you could do is tell me why you want to see him," Nelson complained.

"I'll do that. I want to see him because I think you're a darned good baseball player," and Ted refused to explain further.

It seemed to Ted that in the confusion of the crowd at that Class A game on Monday, Ken Kutler had introduced him to a Mr. Ream. It was not until afterward that he realized this must be Kyle Ream, the famous Chicago sports writer. If he was still in Forestdale—and Ted had some recollection that he had said he would be there all week—Ted thought it would be very useful to talk with him.

The desk clerk rang Mr. Ream's room. The sports writer said that he remembered Ted, and invited him up. After greeting Ted and asking him to be seated, he inquired:

"Well, what can I do for you, Ted?"

"I understand that you knew Jack Hart pretty well, didn't you?"

"I covered his team while he was on it, if that's what you mean."

"Would you mind telling me more about him? I'm interested in knowing what sort of person he is."

"I see," said Mr. Ream thoughtfully. He looked at Ted shrewdly. "Is this for publication?"

Ted's interview with Hart was already on the presses and could not be changed. "No, it's off the record."

Mr. Ream leaned back in his chair and looked up toward the ceiling. "Yes, I knew Hart. I was with the team at spring training the first year he showed up, a brash young rookie. A rookie is ordinarily a little bit hesitant, a little bit shy—but not Hart. He was good and knew it. Well, some managers admire that kind of spirit, and he was given every chance to show what he could do. As it turned out he could do plenty, so that I'm not going to say he was wrong. By his very brashness he may have earned himself a chance that he wouldn't otherwise have gotten, or at least not so soon.

"He made good in the majors right from the beginning. He was said to be the most promising young player in the league. And soon he was perhaps the most disliked player in the league. Arguments with umpires were routine. Every decision that went against him seemed to be a personal affront, and he was thrown out of more games than any other pitcher I ever saw. It was soon common knowledge that if he could be made angry enough, he was good for nothing, and before long the other players were making a practice of baiting him. He claimed later that it was not his habit to use the brush-back pitch, but I watched the team for years, and the duster was a prominent item in his repertoire. He quarreled with newspapermen, frequently broke training rules, got mixed up in brawls, and had fines and suspensions.

"I made a special effort to understand young Jack Hart. I learned that he grew up with hardships. A major league career had always been his goal, and he strove for it with every ounce of skill and strength and purpose–and I may even say trick–that he possessed. As you know, if you clutch at something too hard it may break, and I think that is what finally happened to his career.

"That he failed to fulfill his earlier promise was not entirely his fault. His record of victories was unimpressive. He played with a tail-end team, and lost many close games that he might have won with a better team behind him. Then there was his shoulder trouble that put him out for long periods. At other times I think he was pitching when his shoulder was bad but he wasn't telling anybody about it. No one ever doubted his courage. But from the money point of view his career was a disappointment to him. It was too short, he was with a losing team, there was no World Series money, he didn't qualify for the better pensions.

"A year ago last spring he was a holdout. I don't take sides in disputes of that kind. The owners claim that a losing team can't afford the pay scales of the better teams. The players' motto is, 'Pay me or trade me.' I suppose it depends mostly on which side of the desk you're sitting on. When Hart finally reported, spring training was half over, and he was overweight and out of condition. He had a poor spring, though that was nothing unusual with him since he was known to be a slow starter. But the word began to move along the grapevine: Hart isn't going to make it this year. He surprised everyone by pitching well in three games. Then he was given a bad time on his next start. It was one of those days when he didn't have anything on the ball, but the manager left him in anyway to take his lumps. That night he was given his release. No other team picked him up, and that was the end of Hart's career in the major leagues. Any questions?"

"If he had three good games and one bad one, why was

he let go? That's not a bad percentage, and apparently he still had something on the ball."

"All I can say is that I don't think he was let go because of his rough housing. And his arm didn't appear to be in such bad shape that some team wouldn't take a chance on him. So of course the rumor mills began to grind, just as they had been grinding for some months past. It was said, and I believe it myself, that the owners had just been waiting for him to have a bad day on the mound so they would have an excuse to get rid of him.

"As to the reason, you can take your choice of rumors, but the most likely one is that he was mixed up with a gambling ring. I don't mean that he was throwing games, and knowing Hart as I do it is impossible for me to suspect him of that. But he did have associates among gamblers, and the story was that he was feeding them tips—all for a heavy price, no doubt. Now you know that reporters do the best possible job in covering their team. But they know some things they don't mention in type—things they feel might hurt the team or which they have promised to keep confidential, or feel are too personal for print. But there is also a lot of gossip around the club house that the reporter never gets onto. Maybe a player's arm is hurting him like the devil, but he may not want the manager to know, and he certainly doesn't want the opposition to know. If you were betting on horse races, it would help if you could talk with each horse before the race and find out how he was feeling and what was on his mind. You can't do that with horses, but you can with people. These were the items the gamblers wanted out of Hart, and which he was probably supplying to them.

"So much for Jack Hart—and I wouldn't have told you this much if I hadn't had a word from Ken Kutler about you. Not that you could put any of this in print anyway, the laws of libel being what they are. So where is Hart now?"

"I believe he left town last evening or this morning."

"And I take it from your interest in the man that he's been muddying the waters around here?"

"I don't know," said Ted wearily, getting to his feet. "I'm just pretty sure that someone has been muddying them."

He thanked Mr. Ream, and left the hotel. He got in beside Nelson, and they drove off, out into the country, neither of them speaking for a while, until Nelson complained:

"You'd better do your thinking out loud if you want me to tune in on your brain waves. Going to tell me whom you met at the hotel?"

"A sports writer who knew Jack Hart pretty well. I told you I didn't think you were so bad batting against Hart. It just seemed to me that he was pretty good—good enough to be in the majors even today. I think his shoulder trouble was a myth, or at least exaggerated. I wanted to find out why he wasn't in the majors, and this sports writer suggested a reason. Hart was widely suspected of having gambling associations."

"Wow!" was Nelson's reaction. "And you think he's still at it, and that was why he was down here?"

"I don't know—but if he was, what team, what players was he interested in? Did he really have a hold on some players, and if so, which ones? I'd like to know the answer to those questions before tomorrow."

16 The Miscreants

"Let's try to see as much of the whole picture as we can," Ted suggested as they drove along. "To begin with, we know that Mr. Scotch is a professional gambler. Ken tipped me off; we figured it out that Mr. Scotch was the person he had in mind and finally Mr. Wyatt admitted it. We also see a possibility that Jack Hart was in with him."

"Now let's take it easy there, Ted," said Nelson cautiously. "All we have against Hart is his past reputation."

"What better evidence is there to go on? If a person did a certain thing in the past, he's likely to do it again. We don't have any reason to believe that Hart reformed. The tough breaks he got would probably have had the effect of hardening him, of making him all the more determined and ruthless. However, I must admit that we have no real evidence against either Mr. Scotch or Mr. Hart.

"Then let's go on to the players themselves. What evidence do we have that any of them may have been tied in with the gamblers? We do know that something peculiar happened at the Eaglet-Typhoon game. Larry and Cal went to it in high spirits, and came back completely crushed. Something must have happened during the game, possibly something that made them suspicious about what was going on. Whatever it was must have involved their own players."

"Why is that, Ted? Why not the Typhoons?"

"Because of the way they refused to talk. I think if they had suspected something about the Typhoons they would have been willing to talk with Mr. Ingram about it, or possibly with me. But their refusal to talk suggests a loyalty to their own player

128

or players. They really didn't know where to turn. Now who could these players have been? I suggest that it must be some of the more prominent players on the team, because gamblers certainly wouldn't be interested in lesser players who might have no chance to influence the outcome of the game, who might even be benched. I would also suggest that these boys would also be players to whom Larry and Cal looked up. That was one of the things that hit them so badly."

"Wait a minute, Ted," said Nelson. "I can see where this is leading. But we're still going to need some proof."

"I did notice one little thing. You took pictures at the game. One of the pictures was of Simon Hartrack at bat—we didn't use the picture, because he struck out anyway with the bases loaded. He's certainly not the only player who ever struck out with the bases loaded, so that's not suspicious in itself, although if you think back, you might get the impression that he was showboating it a little, trying to make it look good. But what struck me about that picture, taken just about as the ball was to be pitched, is that Simon seems to be looking up at the stands instead of toward the pitcher. And if I try to imagine what he was looking at, it would be toward the approximate place where Mr. Scotch was sitting."

"With a few hundred people in those stands, Ted, that's not very good evidence."

"No, it's just a shot in the dark. But the fact is that he did strike out in a pinch. The fact is, also, that Jan Allaine was having a pretty rough day. Well, the game went on. Every time the Eaglets went ahead, it seemed the Typhoons would rally and almost catch up. Then there was Simon's rather surprising throw in the last inning, which let in two runs."

"But if they were trying to throw the game, Ted, they certainly didn't make it."

"No, but maybe they weren't supposed to throw it. They might merely have been acting under instructions to keep down the point spread."

"I've got an objection to that, Ted. Jan and Simon are known to be sworn enemies."

"Are they? They were good friends once. Just supposing they were going into something like this together. Wouldn't it be a good idea for them to pretend to be enemies? Then no one would suspect them of a conspiracy."

"Isn't it possible, Ted, that just one of them is in on it?"

"It's conceivable, but I see certain objections. One point is that if the gamblers wanted to be sure of controlling a game, they might want more than one player under their thumb. In baseball it might be too difficult for one person to throw the game, or limit the point spread. Besides, a pitcher and a catcher make a good team for that purpose. It might be difficult, for example, for a pitcher to throw the game without the catcher knowing what he was doing. And quite possibly the other way around, too.

"But I have a more convincing argument than this. You see, Simon and Jan were rooming together. I imagine it would be very difficult for one of them to sneak out, without the other one knowing it. And we know that two boys did break into the office. It seems that they must have done it together."

"What did they want in the office, Ted?"

"We can't be sure, but it must have had something to do with the baseball records. Have I made a good case yet?"

"You've convinced me that if one of them was in it, the other probably was, too. But how do we know these two are the only ones, Ted?"

Ted frowned. "That's the most difficult and unpleasant part about this thing—you never know where to stop being suspicious. But surely the gamblers have some limits, too. Every player they bribe involves an additional risk of discovery. They wouldn't want to go too far, and if they had the first-string battery under control—particularly since these persons in the amateur games tend to be pretty good batters, too—they might hope that that was enough. If eventually it proves not to be, they may have no choice but to shrug it off. Even gamblers don't win all the time."

"What about other teams, Ted?"

"We can't tell there, either. All we can say is that we don't have any evidence that any other team was involved. Actually it might not matter too much what they did elsewhere, provided we can stick them with *this* job."

"But can we do that, Ted? If Simon and Jan were bribed, what proof have you got to link them with Hart and Scotch? What kind of link would you need?"

"I think I know," said Ted slowly. "On one side of the picture we suspect Jack Hart and Mr. Scotch. On the other side we suspect Simon and Jan. If we could just show some connection between these boys and these men, some past association, wouldn't that be pretty convincing proof?"

Nelson nodded thoughtfully. "I guess it would. But how are you going to establish the connection?"

"The easiest thing to do is to ask Mr. Ingram. Then if he knows of such a connection, we'll tell him the whole story."

Nelson turned the car into a side road which would take them on a little circuit back to Forestdale. "And where do we find Mr. Ingram at this time of the afternoon?"

"Probably at Eastgate. If not we'll try Westgate, and if not there, the hotel."

Ted's first guess proved correct. He had no trouble finding Mr. Ingram in the stands at Eastgate. Much mystified, the manager followed Ted to the car where Nelson was waiting.

"Mr. Ingram," Ted began, "I have a question for you that may sound foolish, but it's really very important. Did any of your players know or meet Jack Hart, before coming to Forestdale?"

"Why, yes. We sent two of our boys up to his baseball clinic in Stanton over a year ago."

"Which boys were they?"

"Our best players, the ones we thought earned the trip and could profit the most–Jan Allaine and Simon Hartrack."

Ted and Nelson exchanged significant glances. "My information is," Ted went on, "that these boys are enemies. Is it possible that their enmity dated back to the time of that trip to Stanton?"

"Why, come to think of it, it might have happened about that time. You boys seem to know a good deal more about this than I do. Just what is it that you know or suspect?"

There seemed no further reason to hold back, and Ted plunged in, revealing the whole story as they had figured it out. Mr. Ingram's face grew increasingly grave as Ted spoke. When Ted had finished, he said:

"What you say isn't exactly proof, Ted, but it certainly is highly indicative. I think the three of us had better go and have a talk with these boys. If there is any possibility that you may be right, we want to stop this thing before it goes any further."

They tried the home where the two boys were staying and found them there. Their hostess showed them up to the boys' room, and left them. Jan and Simon looked deeply troubled, as well as anxious over what was to take place.

Mr. Ingram looked at the boys very seriously. "I have just one question for you two boys, and my advice to you is to answer just as truthfully as you know how. What did you expect to do in the game tomorrow?"

The pitcher and catcher looked at each other, as though each hoped that the other would speak. It was clear that they had something serious on their minds, but were undecided how much to tell. Finally Jan spoke cautiously, but with a tremor in his voice:

"I was hoping that maybe you wouldn't ask me to pitch tomorrow, Mr. Ingram."

"Why, Jan, is there something wrong with your arm?" He looked at the pitcher closely. "No, it isn't your arm, is it? Was there some other reason why you couldn't give your best?"

As though suddenly feeling too much of the burden was being laid upon his partner, Simon spoke up.

"We *wanted* to give our best. Maybe we could give our best, and still do what those people wanted us to do. If our team didn't get too far ahead—"

He stopped suddenly, realizing he had said too much.

"What people, Simon?" asked Mr. Ingram, turning upon him.

Simon hesitated, and then apparently decided that the best course was to tell everything.

"Those gamblers—the ones who wanted us to keep the score down. Anyway, they told us that was all they wanted. Then yesterday we found out differently."

"But we certainly weren't going to throw the game!" Jan burst in. "We told each other all day today that no matter what happened to us, we weren't going to throw the game away. They told us we'd never have to do that, that all they expected of us was to shave runs. Then yesterday we got the word: they want us to lose!"

"All right," said Mr. Ingram quietly. "Let's all sit down."

The two boys sat down on one bed, Ted and Nelson on the other, and Mr. Ingram took the only chair in the room.

"Now boys, when did this business begin?"

"Last year, about two weeks before the play-offs," said Jan.

"And you were told the most number of runs you could win by?"

"Yes."

"We had three close games in the play-offs last year," Mr. Ingram informed the older boys. "But we managed to win each of them. Our battery performed at less than par, but that was easily excused on the basis that they were overworked and tired." He turned his attention back to the players. "Then did you do any point shaving this season?"

"Oh, no," said Simon, shaking his head. "They weren't interested in the regular games–just the play-offs. We hoped we would never hear from them again, but they got in touch with us again, about two weeks before the play-offs, just like last year."

"How many runs were you allowed to win by this year?"

"Two runs, in each of the first two games."

"I see." Mr. Ingram nodded. "Then you just made it, didn't you?"

"Yes, but I had to make that crummy throw in the seventh to do it, and that looked awful. And then last night they told me we had to lose tomorrow's game."

"But we weren't going to do it!" Jan broke in wildly. "We didn't mind shaving points so much, although we knew it was risky–but we couldn't throw the game, not deliberately just like that. The other guys were counting on us. Simon said we should offer to give them back the money, but I knew it wouldn't do any good. They don't care about a little money. They want to spend a little money to make a lot of money."

"Now who were these men you were dealing with?" asked Mr. Ingram.

"We don't know! We never saw them. We just got a telephone call last year, and they told us where to call them, and when. And they told us what our point spread was, and where we should pick up the money. It was always there–even after the game was over, so we knew they were honest that way. Then it was the same thing this year. Last night we called this number we were supposed to call, and they told us about losing."

"A private number?" asked Ted quickly.

"Maybe–I don't know. It was just the number they gave us."

"Did you always talk to the same man?"

"I don't know whether it was always the same one or not.

Sometimes Simon called, and sometimes I called. We didn't talk to them often enough to tell."

"Simon, didn't you take a look up at the stands while you were at bat with the bases loaded yesterday?" Nelson questioned him.

"Sure, I did. But I didn't know who the man was. They just told me that somebody would be up there watching us. It was sort of like a threat."

"What have you boys done with the money you received?" Mr. Ingram continued.

"It's in a bank account in a different town. We never spent any of it."

"Do your parents know about it?"

"Oh, no. I don't know what they'd do if they found out about it. They'd probably disown us, I guess."

"And you were the boys who broke into the baseball office last Sunday night?"

The boys looked at each other unhappily. Perhaps they had hoped that this one detail, at least, would not come out.

"Yes," Simon admitted. "We were arguing about how we'd shaved the runs last year, and we couldn't remember exactly what we did. We wanted to be careful not to do the same thing this year because someone might suspect us. Some of the scouts look over those records pretty carefully. Anyway, we didn't want to look any worse than we had to because some of those scouts might be interested in *us*. That's why we wanted to look over last year's records, but that man with the flashlight scared us away before we found them."

"We didn't think it was so bad," said Jan eagerly, "because it was an empty building, and we didn't have guns, and we weren't going to take anything."

"It was a serious offense just the same, boys. Just one final question: are there any other boys in this thing besides yourselves?"

They shook their heads. "Nobody that we know of," Simon

assured him. "Anyway, we're sure there's no one else on our team."

"Well, boys," said Mr. Ingram, getting up, "you've made a pretty good mess of things. My first step will be to notify your parents and ask them to come up here."

"Do you have to?" asked Jan, more upset than at any moment since they had entered the room.

"I'm afraid I do. It's altogether too serious a matter for me to gloss over. And then I will have to discuss the matter with the police."

"We confessed, and we're willing to give the money back," Simon pointed out. "Do we have to have police records, too?"

"I can't see any help for it. In the first place, there's a police charge already—this matter of breaking and entering a building. The police are still investigating the matter. They know there were only a few teams in town last Sunday night. They may turn up some further clue that will point to you, or the man who frightened you away may be able to make a kind of identification after all. And since Ted here was able to figure this matter out, and a number of people already know it, we can't tell but what other people will learn of it or figure it out for themselves. It won't do to leave a threat like that hanging over your heads.

"In the second place there is the matter of the money, which must somehow be disposed of. I have no authority to decide about that.

"And in the third place, if you expect matters to go easier for you, you must be willing to cooperate with the police. It is important to stop the men who were bribing you. The police will need all the help you can give them, and may even need your testimony at a future trial. You see how impossible it would be to hope for secrecy. However, I will try to arrange things just as promptly and quietly as I can. And Ted, may we have your cooperation along that line, too?"

"Oh, yes. Mr. Dobson never publishes the names of juvenile

offenders, and he never even describes the crime unless it is a matter of public record."

"But all the guys will know about it, won't they?" asked Jan.

"I guess they will," replied Mr. Ingram. "You're beginning to think about that just one year too late."

17 The Verdict of the Court

Now that they knew the story was out, Larry and Cal were eager to talk, relieved at last of the burden of the secret they were carrying.

"Here's how I caught on," Larry explained. "You know, sometimes, when the whole crowd is shouting, and suddenly they all stop at once, you find you've been talking louder than you realized? That was when I heard Simon say to Jan that he was going to strike out. I whispered to Cal, and he said he thought he heard it, too, but that we must have misunderstood him. Well, then, Simon went up to the plate with the bases loaded, and he *did* strike out. Of course, it might just have happened that way, you know–maybe it started out as a joke, or something. But anyway that made us both suspicious."

"That's when we began to watch Simon and Jan closely," Cal went on, "and it sure seemed to me that Simon wasn't calling for Jan's best pitches when he should. It was something that maybe we wouldn't have paid any attention to if it hadn't been for what we overheard."

"And I was watching Jan, too," Larry picked up, "and it seemed to me that every once in a while he was grooving the pitch. If I hadn't been suspicious already, I would have thought he was just tired."

"But Simon's bad throw in the seventh inning settled all that," Cal concluded. "Then we knew for sure that they were trying to throw the game, and we didn't know what to do. Even if we told, who would believe us?"

"Not exactly throw it," Ted corrected. "They just wanted to

138

keep the score down." He paused a moment. "What do you suppose made them do it?"

"College," said Larry firmly. "They both want to be scientists, and they must have been trying to save up enough to get to college. I want to go to college, too, but I'm hoping I can get a scholarship or a loan if I can't make it any other way. The trouble is that you don't know about those things for sure until the last minute–you can't plan ahead. But I wouldn't take any money from gamblers."

"I wouldn't either," Cal agreed. "What good is money if you're in jail, or your parents don't like you any more, or you haven't any friends?"

"I understand Jan and Simon went to Stanton a year ago to attend Jack Hart's baseball clinic," said Ted casually. "Did they have anything to say about it when they got back?"

"Oh, yes," Larry recollected. "They had a swell time, and said Hart was a great guy. He showed them a lot of inside baseball stuff. And he told them about watching out for themselves if they had a chance. He said if they were football or basketball players they would probably have a lot of scholarship chances, but because they were baseball players they probably wouldn't. That was why they had to watch out for their big chance when it came, to make sure they didn't lose it."

Larry saw no hidden significance in the conversation he was relating. Neither he nor Cal suspected Jack Hart's possible involvement with the gambling ring, nor had Jan and Simon. On the basis of the skimpy evidence he possessed so far, Ted had no intention of enlightening them.

"What do you think will happen to Hart, Ted?" asked Nelson, when they were alone.

"We don't know yet whether the police will get enough evidence to convict him of anything. I imagine he was just an advance scout for the gamblers. He talked with possible victims, easily won their confidence, and then if he found a likely prospect, handed the name on to the gamblers. Weeks or months later the boy might get a call, but he would have no reason to associate that with Hart. But the police are onto his way of operating now, and wherever he goes his record will follow him. It isn't as important to punish these people as it is to put a stop to their operations."

Late in the evening Mr. Ingram called to say that he had arranged a meeting with Judge Harder in juvenile court for eleven-thirty the next morning.

"We'll want you there as a witness, Ted, and I suppose Nelson ought to come, too, since he can back up your story if necessary. The boys' parents will all be there, too."

Ted relayed this information to Nelson, who agreed to come. Mr. Ingram did not wish Larry or Cal to attend, but said he was calling a baseball meeting for their team at twelve-thirty at the council hall, where he would reveal to them whatever details he thought necessary. In the meantime he asked Larry and Cal to say nothing.

Mr. Dobson's first news of these events was given to him by Ted at the office the next morning. Strangely enough, the editor was not as disturbed about it as Ted had expected.

"It was that breaking into the office which bothered me the most, Ted. It had a sinister ring to it, and I'm very glad that's been cleared up. Actually the situation seems less serious than I had a feeling it might be, and I've no doubt we've nipped it in the bud. I don't think these gamblers got very far with very many boys—yet. By the way, have you seen Ken's story?"

Ted had not, but now he had time to look it over. It was a big front-page display in which Ken disclosed the interest of professional gamblers in the tournament taking place in Forestdale. Ken seemed to know all the odds and point spreads on each team, and how these had changed as the teams' fortunes improved. He did not name the man he believed to be at the head of the ring, though there was a suggestion that he knew who it was. Perhaps Ted and Nelson—and now Mr. Dobson—

were the only readers who would be aware that the man he was talking about was Mr. Scotch.

In a way, Ken had a scoop where Ted did not. But still Ted had some information which he believed Ken did not possess, including the possibility of Jack Hart's involvement, and of course the actual bribery of two players. Unless these matters were revealed publicly following the juvenile-court hearing, Mr. Dobson would never print them. This was one time Ted was glad he did not have a story.

With a little time to spare at last, Ted could at least get out to the Rangers' game at Eastgate, meeting Nelson there by pre-arrangement. There was a good crowd at the field in spite of the early hour.

The Rangers were obliged to rely on Murdock again, and he was not as sharp as he might have been had he not pitched on Wednesday. The Bearcats seemed to hit him freely, though with poor luck at first. Then they slowly began to pick up a run here and a run there, until their lead became formidable.

The Rangers, in their turn, had little luck against the Bearcats' pitcher—the same pitcher they had used Monday evening, but had rested since. He had all the equipment he needed for their classification, and seemed to be headed for even better things next season.

There was no repetition of the bean-ball incidents. One pitch did come fairly close to the head of a Ranger batter, but it was a curve ball that had obviously gotten away from the pitcher, and no one made any protest.

The Bearcats' pitcher went on in full command of the situation, mowing the batters down, many of them on strikeouts. He gave up only three singles and one walk, and the game ended with the score six to nothing in their favor.

No one had to make any apologies for the Forestdale team. They had gone far with only one good pitcher on their staff, making a battle of it right down to the last game. They got up off the bench to walk across the field and congratulate the victors. The applause of the crowd was meant as much for them as it was for the Stanton team.

"Things never do turn out quite the way they ought to, do they?" Nelson remarked, as he and Ted walked toward his car, with just about enough time to make the juvenile-court hearing.

"Maybe this one did. Stanton really does have a good, solid team. They found they can win without resorting to dirty tactics. That ought to be a lesson to them—and maybe to other teams as well. By the way, did you hear that the Bohunks won their game at Westgate this morning?"

Judge Harder convened the hearing in his private chambers. The proceedings were informal. No oaths were required, and no written record of the testimony was taken. Noticing Ted, he said:

"You realize, Ted, that you are here as a witness, and not as a newspaper reporter?"

"Yes, Your Honor."

The judge questioned the two boys about all that had happened, uncovering the details which were for the most part already known to Ted, Nelson and Mr. Ingram. The boys both denied that they knew the names of the men with whom they had been dealing. The parents were also questioned, and, obviously shocked, all denied that they had had any inkling of what was going on.

"Does anyone have anything else to say?" the judge inquired.

Ted felt moved to speak. It seemed to him that there were a few matters which had not been sufficiently brought out in the testimony so far.

"May I say a few words, Your Honor?"

"Please do, Ted."

"Just one or two details. I don't think anyone has mentioned yet that the reason these boys wanted the money was for their college educations. I think this makes their motive at least a little more understandable.

"My other point is that I believe these boys were encouraged by a former baseball star in whom they had a great deal of confidence. He urged them to take their big chance when it came, without quite telling them what their big chance was going to involve. And I am sure that these gamblers, too, had a smooth line of talk, trying persuasion at first, and as a last resort turning to threats."

"Do you have evidence against these men, Ted?"

"Not evidence that would hold up in court, Your Honor."

"But evidence which might be valuable to the police in conducting their own investigation?"

"I believe so."

"Then I will not ask you to disclose the names of these men in court, Ted, but I do instruct you to give all the information you possess to the police, and work with them as closely as you can in this matter."

He made a few notations on a paper, then asked Jan and Simon to stand up before his desk.

"I have no doubt that you fully understand the seriousness of what you have done. It is in my power to fine you, to sentence you to a term on a boys' farm, or even remove you from the custody of your parents. However, it is not the purpose of these proceedings to punish you, but rather to find what can be done to help you while still preserving the rights of the society in which you live.

"Besides the criminal acts which you have committed, you have betrayed the trust of your parents, the loyalty of your comrades, and your own standard of ethics. Although the evidence would indicate that the relationship with your parents was a little looser than desirable—a situation which they may now desire to correct—I do not hold your parents responsible.

"I order that you be placed on probation for a period of one year. Arrangements will be made for you to report to an officer in your own community. The money in your bank account is to be turned over to Mr. Ingram, who in turn will donate it to the baseball scholarship fund. You may eventually become eligible yourselves for a grant or loan from this fund, but if you get it, it will be because you deserve it. With respect to participation by you in your championship baseball game this afternoon, I will make no ruling, but leave the matter to the discretion of the baseball authorities. The case is dismissed."

As Ted was about to leave the courtroom, Jan went up to him.

"Thanks for speaking up for us, Ted. I don't think the judge would have let us off with probation, if you hadn't."

"I tried to understand your reasoning," said Ted soberly. "Your situation was like quicksand. It looks all right to begin with, but soon you're in deeper than you had realized, and there doesn't seem to be any way to get out."

18　Soaring Eagles

Though they had won the verdict in court, the boys did not win it with their teammates. Mr. Ingram had previously scheduled a meeting of all the players. Since Larry and Cal already knew most of the story, and since there seemed little chance of hushing up the matter indefinitely, he decided that the rest of the team was entitled to hear the facts, too. He explained the matter simply, then put it up to them to decide whether Jan and Simon should play in the big game.

Fiery Eddie Youngman took the floor.

"We are sure surprised to learn that two players on our team were shaving points in our three tournament games last year, and in our two games so far this year. We were in trouble in each game, and almost lost them. Maybe if Jan and Simon had shaved any more, we *would* have lost them. Now we have to decide whether we want those same two players to play today. Mr. Ingram says they'd *like* to play, but how do we know they're not afraid of the gamblers, and will do their best?

"So far all I've heard is promises. They were caught, and they promised that they'll never do it again. Well, I'm willing to give them another chance–next year–to show what they will do. But right now I want something more than promises. We can go into this game with a pair of second-stringers who we know will give it everything they've got. Or we can go in with this pair who've been playing a different kind of game than we knew about. My vote goes to the second-stringers. So the gamblers want us to lose, and maybe we'll be playing into their hands by using our second-stringers. Or maybe we'll just have a little surprise for them. What do you say?"

A chorus of approval greeted this speech, and the boys voted to expel Jan and Simon from the team. They were not even allowed to put on their uniforms or sit on the bench, but watched the game from the stands.

Ted looked around for Mr. Scotch, but could not see him. It was probable that Ken's story had driven him out of town if nothing else had. The police had Mr. Scotch's private number traced by now, but it might be more difficult to find the man. Keeping an eye on Jack Hart might lead them to him.

As Nelson watched Larry Dodge warming up, he exclaimed:

"How do you like that fast ball? I've watched him warm up before, and I didn't know he could throw that hard."

"No," Ted agreed, "and I'll bet he didn't know it, either."

With their second-stringers in action, the Eaglets were definitely underdogs, but they never gave the slightest indication of it. Ted had seen determined teams before, but never one as grimly determined as this one.

In their first turn at bat they drove to the attack. Two runs were scored by solid hits, skillful base running, and alert team play. Then Larry came to the hill for the last half of the inning. He struck out the first batter, got the second on a soft grounder, and the third on a pop. And this proved to be the pattern of the game. Larry never eased up on a single pitch, not even late in the game. And Cal, behind the plate, seemed to be doing a clever job of mixing his signals.

There were hits, for Larry was not as gifted a pitcher as Jan, but the team behind him was fired up, and kept him from grief with their steady and occasionally spectacular play. The Eaglets carried a three-to-nothing lead into the last half of the seventh inning, and that was the way the game ended.

"Well, I guess those Eaglets really soared today," was Nelson's remark as he and Ted left the field.

"Maybe we'd better stop calling them Eaglets. They ought to be full-fledged eagles after the way they earned their wings today. I hope we'll have another chance to see them soar. I'm a little curious to see how this whole thing comes out."

Nelson unlocked the rear door of his car, wanting to put his camera in there. He stopped, as he spotted something on the floor.

"Well, what do you know?" he exclaimed, picking up a model airplane. It was obviously the one that had been stolen from the races, and was still in good condition.

"Why did you do it, Nel?" asked Ted mockingly, and then more seriously, "Do you have any idea who put it there?"

"No, not exactly. But only once today did I leave my car open for a little while, and I know what team was hanging around, and I think I might even be able to pick out the right boy if I put my mind to it. Why bother? He went to some risk to return it when he could just as easily have smashed it up. As long as he's had a change of heart, why don't we forget it?"

"That's all right with me," Ted declared, getting into the front seat. "I'm bushed. I've had enough for one week."

"You mean you don't even have enough energy left to come to the victory parade tonight, with the floats and bands, and dancing and marshmallow roast afterward?"

Ted brightened. "You know something? All at once I'm not tired any more."

Nelson started the engine. "I've got to admit I'm disappointed about Jack Hart, though. He gave the boys lots of good advice about baseball and stuff like that."

"Sure, but he forgot to give them the best advice of all."

"What's that, Ted?"

"Never have anything to do with professional gamblers."